Y0-BRS-746

They were getting to the demand for blood. . .

The priestess bit her lower lip and braced herself as she stared down at the frightened sacrifice. The two girls were almost the same age. The priestess, Humming Bird, felt sorry for the other girl. But they needed rain. She raised the knife, the torch lights gleaming on the green beetle-wing bracelets around her tawny naked arms. And then all hell broke loose.

The carved stone wall, after standing over a thousand years, exploded inwards as Captain Gringo crashed through it, using his helmeted head as a battering ram. . .

Novels by Ramsay Thorne

Published by
WARNER BOOKS

Renegade #13

THE MAHOGANY PIRATES

by

Ramsay Thorne

WARNER BOOKS

A Warner Communications Company

WARNER BOOKS EDITION

Copyright © 1982 by Lou Cameron
All rights reserved.

Warner Books, Inc.,
75 Rockefeller Plaza,
New York, N.Y. 10019

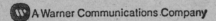 A Warner Communications Company

Printed in the United States of America

First Printing: June, 1982

10 9 8 7 6 5 4 3 2 1

Their lives were saved by the Chinese cook aboard the *Serpiente*. This was not because the wayward Oriental was a hero or even a good cook. The little coastal schooner couldn't afford to hire a good cook or even a matching set of sails. So as it wallowed down the Mosquito Coast in a heavy ground swell, Captain Gringo lay in his bunk as sick as a dog. The tall blond soldier of fortune seldom got sea sick and the seas weren't all that bad that morning in any case. But as he lay there wondering how you said "bicarbonate of soda" to a Chinese who didn't speak as much Spanish as he did, the miserable American knew he was going to throw up. So with a grimace he swung off the bunk and went out on deck to get it over with.

At the rail he found his side-kick, Gaston, already feeding the fish with his own greasy supper. Captain Gringo muttered, "Mind if I join you?" and heaved over the side.

As the two of them leaned there, feeling lousy, Gaston sighed and said, "We are going to have to murder that maniac in the galley before he kills us both, my old and rare! We face at least three more days to Limon aboard this tripple-titted species of a vessel!"

Captain Gringo gagged, saw nothing important was left to come up, and wiped a hand across his face before he muttered, "Don't look at me. It was your idea to book

5

passage on this tub. I thought you said the skipper was an old pal of yours."

"*Merde alors,* how was I to know the man had the digestive system of a camel, Dick? What in God's name do you imagine that crazed Chinese cooked those noodles in last night, hein?"

"I'm trying to decide if it was naphtha soap or coal oil. I think we'd better teach him to make sandwiches."

The tall American took an experimental gasp of sea air and decided he was going to live. He glanced toward the east to see what time it was, but the early morning sun was hidden in the thin fog above the rolling swells. He asked, "Have you got the time, Gaston? I left my watch in the cabin." Then he saw Gaston was standing in his bare feet and skivvies, too, and added, "Sorry. Dumb question."

"*Oui,* one advantage of a voyage on a small smuggler is that one does not have to consider one's appearance before the other passengers, since there are no other passengers. I am beginning to feel better. Would you care to join me for breakfast?"

"Hey, come on, I don't want to puke again. It's kind of chilly out here in this morning fog. I think I'll try for some more shut-eye. I hardly slept a wink last night, thanks to that God-awful grub."

He turned from the rail just in time to see something looming high above them between the sails of the schooner and then, as he yelled, "What the hell?" a steamer hit them, hard, amidships!

The schooner was cut in two as it rolled under the big steel bow of the three-island steamer, but Captain Gringo didn't notice. The impact had thrown him over the far side and, as he held his breath and tried to fight his way to the surface, one of his hands was stung by barnacle-studded steel and he realized he was *under* the steamer. He was being sucked back toward its churning screw, too!

He knew he couldn't swim against the wash, so he dove

deeper into the darkness below the ship, trying not to think of what the blood he was trailing in the water from his injured hand would mean to any friendly neighborhood hammerheads. He knew the big whirling blade above him would do an even faster job on him than any puny shark!

The screw almost got him anyway. He was head down, swimming as hard as he could, but moving the wrong way as the suction from the steamer fought him. Then the water around him grew lighter and, since he was about to drown in any case, he gave up and popped to the surface amid the foam of the steamer's wake. He looked up and saw the name painted on the stern as the big steamer moved away, leaving him bobbing amid shattered planking and other debris from the run over schooner. He spit out a mouthful of brine and headed for a floating hatchcover, wondering if Gaston had made it and if the steamer's crew was going to fish him out before some cruising shark scented the blood from his skinned knuckles.

As he reached the hatchcover he raised his hand from the water and started to kick away from the blood he'd left in the water. He spotted a human head and called out, "Over here! I've got a float!"

As the other swam his way, cursing and spitting, he saw to his relief it was Gaston. Gaston joined him, clinging to the far side, and remarked, conversationally, "How nice to see you again. Would you mind telling me what happened?"

Captain Gringo pointed at the stern of the steamer with his chin and said, "That big freighter ran us down in the fog. But just hang on a minute. It takes a vessel that size a while to turn."

Gaston stared morosely at the steamer, now a gray blur in the fog, and said, "I hate to be a spoilsport, my old and rare, but I do not think they have any intention of stopping."

It was starting to look that way to the tall American,

too. "Aw, shit," Captain Gringo replied, "they have to know they hit us, even if we were a rather small vessel. That was a hell of a bump. Do you see any other survivors?"

"*Mais non.* Aside from the helmsman, I do not think anyone else was on deck at the moment of impact. One gathers the poor individual at the helm was not a swimmer, hein?"

"The bastards! The no-good-stupid bastards!"

"Let us be fair, Dick. The rest of the crew were no doubt *très* confused to awaken under water and upside down, non?"

"I'm not talking about *our* side, dammit! That fucking steamer isn't heaving to! They ran us down and just steamed on, like a wagon running over a lizard in the road!"

"*Oui,*" Gaston sighed, "one gathers they did not wish to get involved? I am an old soldier, not a sea dog, but it seems to me I heard, somewhere, that a vessel under sail has the right of way over a steam-powered ship. Our hit-and-run steamship captain no doubt wishes to avoid tedious discussions with the maritime authorities regarding his master's papers, hein?"

Captain Gringo nodded grimly and growled, "I'll have something to say about that bastard's seamanship as soon as we get ashore! I read that tub's name and homeport off their transom. It's the *Imperial Trader,* out of Liverpool. Goddamn Limey bastards think they own the whole damned ocean!"

Gaston looked around as a ground swell lifted them and then he sighed and said, "I admire your American optimism, Dick. Aside from the fact that the two of us are wanted by the law, have you noticed we seem to be bobbing about in the middle of this ocean you accuse the British of hogging?"

"Yeah, we're going to have to make our way ashore. It's hard to tell in this haze, but I think the coast must be over that way. Let me work around to your side and we'll kick this hatch cover in that direction."

As he joined Gaston on the seaward side, the older and smaller Frenchman muttered, "*Merde alors,* you species of idiot! We must be fifty kilometers or more from the Mosquito Coast in the first place and, in the second, I fear we are off Nicaragua!"

"So? What do you suggest? That Goddamn steamer's not coming back and nobody else knows we're here. Start kicking, damn it!"

Gaston did so, but protested, "This strikes me as a *très fatigue* way to march to one's execution, my old and rare. Have you forgotten we are wanted dead or alive in Nicaragua?"

"No. Remind me not to join the losing side in any more revolutions. There may be a chance we'll fetch ashore along some deserted strip of the coast. We'll die for sure if we don't try. I don't know how long it's going to take the sharks to finish the crew that went down with the schooner, so let's not hang around to find out!"

Gaston started kicking harder as he muttered, "One sees a certain method in your madness, after all, hein. But do you really think we can last that long, Dick? Regard how slowly we seem to be moving this thrice-accursed hatch cover. What if we were to simply start swimming?"

"Sixty kilometers? The English Channel's not a quarter of that and nobody's ever swum it yet!"

"We French prefer to call it La Manche rather than the English Channel," Gaston grimaced, "but your point is well taken. As long as we are indulging ourselves in mad optimism, let's hope we hit one of the many islands off the Mosquito Coast, hein? Some of the coral keys lie well out to sea. They are barren desert islands for the most part, and the ones with water and vegetation tend to be infested by cannibals, but . . ."

"Hey, save your breath and keep kicking," Captain Gringo cut in, adding, "You don't have to cheer me up, you old bastard. We've lost our guns, our money, even our clothes, and the last time we visited Nicaragua everyone

9

was shooting at us. So you can leave out *cannibals*. Okay?"

Gaston shrugged and added, "I think they are called Caribs in any case. Could I have a drink of water, Pappa? This endless toil seems to be making me thirsty."

"Just stick your head under and inhale, you asshole. Can't you do anything without talking a blue streak?"

"Mais non, we French are born conversationalists. It's bad enough I can not move my hands as we struggle with this water-logged species of heavy timber, non?"

Captain Gringo didn't answer. He knew he couldn't shut Gaston up and he was already feeling the effects of the unexpected early morning exercise. He might have felt more up to shoving the hatch cover sixty kilometers if he hadn't started out sick-and-tired to begin with, or if he knew, for sure, that they were really heading for shore.

By high noon it was worse. They were both cramped, thirsty and, now that the sun was shining straight down through the overcast, Gaston could be right that they were going in circles. There was no wind. There was no particular pattern to the sluggish swells as they rode up and down on them clinging to the hatch cover, and they weren't making enough leeway to notice in any case. Gaston groaned, "My legs are killing me. That is the trouble with sharks. They are never about when you need them, hein?"

"I don't think there are any sharks to worry about, right now, Gaston. They'd have had us by this time if there were."

"That is what I mean. I confess I'm too weak willed to just let go of these soggy planks and get it over with. But when one is doomed in any case, I find the suspense *très fatigue*. How long do you imagine we can last, my hyperkinetic youth?"

Captain Gringo stopped kicking as he said, "Take a break. We'd better rest until the sun moves enough to tell us east from west again. If we don't spy land by sundown, it's been nice knowing you. My banged up hand's stopped bleeding and sharks almost never hit at midday. If there's nothing particularly yummy in the water to draw them, they like to hunt at dawn and dusk. So if you suddenly find yourself alone out here toward sundown, forgive my rude departure and try to climb up on the hatch cover. It won't hold me, and it sure won't hold us both, but you're a skinny little bastard, so it's worth a try."

Gaston swore softly in French, as he was too big a boy to scream, and then, as they crested a ground swell, he laughed and said, "Ah, just as I thought I was getting rid of you, too! Look over there, Dick! Am I seeing things or is that not a line of palms on the horizon?"

By the time Captain Gringo could swing around to look they were down in a trough between the swells. But then as they rose, he saw them too, and said, "Siesta's over. Let's get this raft moving, Old Buddy!"

It was easier said than done. It took them almost two hours to reach the breakers, where they abandoned the hatch cover and swam for the shore of the low lying key. As Captain Gringo felt sand under his bare feet he stood up, staggered wearily ashore, and fell face down on the gritty coral beach to recover his breath. Gaston lay a few yards away, moaning. Then, as the tropic sun, despite the overcast, dried them out and began to burn, Captain Gringo sat up and looked around.

There wasn't much to see. The sand was chalk white and littered with broken shards of shell. A hundred yards inland, above the reach of the waves, a ragged line of palmettos formed the only landscape. The tall American muttered, "Shit, if those were coconuts we'd have something to drink. How are you feeling, Gaston?"

The little wirey Frenchman rolled over, spit out some sand and said, "Dead. But I need a drink before you bury me. Do you suppose the nearest cantina serves cerveza on credit?"

Captain Gringo got to his bare feet in his shorts and undershirt as he grimaced and muttered, "I wish you hadn't reminded me of that. Aren't you even packing one of those rubbers stuffed with goodies, like money?"

"*Mais non,* I left my bunk to throw up, not to go on a wild spending spree. All we face the unknown with, this time, is our fair white bodies, and if we don't take them into the shade, we shall soon be red as lobsters, hein?"

They gingerly moved for the tree line over the shell-littered sand. Captain Gringo bent and picked up a thick broken clam shell, testing the sharp edge with his thumb. Gaston nodded, spotted a hefty conch shell, and armed himself as well. They walked into the meager shade between the squat palmettos. The ground was now littered with dry-splintered palm stalks even tougher on bare feet. The strip of vegetation was only about fifty-feet wide before they faced another stretch of dazzling white sand and the same sullen sea. They were indeed on a small coral key. Captain Gringo stared morosely at the far horizon and muttered, "Well, I grew up wanting to play Robinson Crusoe. Ain't this gonna be fun?"

Gaston sniffed and said, "Fun for you, perhaps. I fail to share your Anglo-Saxon enthusiasm for that *très* tedious English novel. You know, of course, the author was a homosexual, hein?"

Captain Gringo walked over to a palmetto and got to work with his clam shell before he asked, "Where did you hear that about poor old Defoe? He wrote *Moll Flanders,* too, and that was a pretty salty book for a sissy to have written."

Gaston shrugged and said, "Perhaps he was bisexual, then. Robinson Crusoe was not the work of a man who enjoyed the company of women. What are you doing to that poor tree?"

"Trying to get you that drink you were asking about. This shell makes a piss-poor knife, but if I can get to the growing tip amid all this dry crap we'll have Heart Of Palm salad for lunch. I must have missed something when I read *Robinson Crusoe* as a kid. I don't remember anything in it about queers."

"You don't? What about Crusoe's native lover, Friday?"

"Shit, Gaston. Friday was his servant, not his lover."

"Oh no? Then tell me, my innocent lad, who *did* Robinson Crusoe make love to all those years on that island? Do you remember the part about how Friday began their relationship by kissing Crusoe's foot? *Très* suspicious, if you ask me!"

Captain Gringo cut six or eight inches of pale green watery palm heart out of the little tree, tore it in two, and handed half to Gaston as he said, "Here, shove this in your mouth and stop talking dirty. I might have known a Frenchman would worry about Robinson Crusoe's sex life."

"What is there to wonder? Had Defoe been a French author, Friday would have been a native *girl*! We do not share the English taste for buggery and . . . hmm, this is not bad. It could use oil and vinegar, but at least we know we shan't die of thirst, hein?"

Captain Gringo looked around as he chewed his own bland palm salad and swallowed pulp and all before he said, "Yeah, we can make a lean-to out of palm fronds, too. But we're going to have to find something more solid to eat if we plan on staying here any length of time."

Gaston wrinkled his nose and said, "I'm ready to leave at once, but I see the wisdom in your dismal words. There is nothing on this key to cause even a wandering Carib to visit it. If there were coconuts, there would be coconut crabs, perhaps. There is no skirting reef, so such fishing as there is promises to be poor, even if we had fishing gear. We could be stuck here for years, Dick, and I just told you I don't share Robinson's taste in bed partners, hein?"

"Jesus H. Christ," Captain Gringo muttered, "nothing to eat, nothing to wear, probably no way to start a fire, and he's worried about bed partners! We haven't even got a *bed*, you asshole!"

"Don't speak to me about my asshole, yet. Perhaps after we have been marooned a few months I may be able to make the mental adjustments. What in the devil do you think you are doing, now?"

Captain Gringo was splitting a green palm leaf with his shell. He said, "This stuff looks pretty stringy. Hope it stays flexible when it's dry."

He twisted his improvised string, tested it, and grunted in satisfaction as he coiled it around his hand, picked up a stick, and proceeded to split it with the sharp shell, explaining, "If this works, I'll have a hatchet. We've plenty of shells, wood, and cordage to work with. Ought to be easy enough to whip together a primitive tool kit."

Gaston shrugged and asked, "Then what? We build a boat? These palmettos do not offer timber, Dick. The logs are weak and light, like balsa."

"Damnit, you want to stay here until we go fruit for each other, or are you going to help me? It shouldn't take us more than a day or so to build a raft. We might be able to make a sail out of palm matting and even if we can't, these palm fronds can serve as paddles, right?"

"*Merde alors,* you can be the boy! I'm not about to trust my delicate curves to that cruel sea again, now I have solid ground under me! We don't even know where we are, you idiot!"

"Sure we do. We're on a desert island off the coast of Central America, and there's not a chance in Hell anyone's going to come looking for us in the foreseeable future. Bust that conch against a tree and see if you can get a sharp edge, damn it."

Gaston swung his shell against a palmetto experimentally and was rewarded with a spongy thunk. Captain Gringo snorted in disgust and said, "Hit it with another shell, you dunce."

So Gaston sat on a fallen log, picked up another thick clam shell, and gave it a try. Then he laughed, "I am a genius! Look what I just did. I have just broken off the tip of my conch and turned the clam shell into a reasonable blade. So now I am rich. I have a fog horn as well as my own little hatchet!"

"Swell, just as the fog's starting to lift and there's not

15

a vessel in sight in any case. We'd better pass on ship building for now and throw up a shelter, Gaston. We're both beginning to look like lobsters."

So they finished whipping their broken shells into wooden handles and got to work on a shelter none too soon. By the time they'd improvised a crude lean-to of sticks and fronds, the afternoon sun was blazing down from the cobalt blue afternoon sky like an open furnace door.

In their weakened condition, the effort had exhausted them. They lay in the shade panting, thirsty again, but too tired to cut out any more palm hearts.

"I am dying for a smoke," Gaston said. "What did Crusoe and Friday puff on, besides each other, hein?"

Captain Gringo smiled thinly and answered, "They had a better island, now that I think back. Crusoe's island was supposed to be somewhere off the tropic coast of the Americas, too, but it seems there was wild tobacco, along with grape vines, orange trees, wild goats and other goodies. Defoe might have cheated a little by letting old Robinson salvage that wrecked ship, too. It might be a little rougher on a real life desert island than it was in that book."

"*Oui,* that is why I still say the author was a pervert. If one is going to provide a castaway with everything from a Garden of Eden to a hardware store, why strand him with a native boy, hein?"

Captain Gringo didn't answer as he picked up a fallen palm frond and stick, and started rubbing them together until he had a groove in the frond. Gaston asked why he was jerking off with such an odd set of tools and the tall American answered, "Beats the shit out of me. I've always heard you can start a fire this way. There must be a knack to it."

"I have seen Indians do it. But it even took them forever. Why do you want a fire, anyway? "We've nothing to smoke or cook and it's hot as the devil, even in this shade."

Captain Gringo nodded and said, "I noticed. That's why I was hoping this crud might be dry enough to set afire by friction. It's hot and dry now, but we have no blankets, we're damned near naked, and you may have noticed it gets cold and clammy when the fog rises after sundown. Aside from that, if we can get a bonfire going on the beach, someone may see it!"

Gaston sat up and said, "Ah, in that case you have my permission to try. Now that I see I have not perished from heat stroke, after all, I shall see if there are clams out there along the water's edge. The tide would seem to be going out, hein?"

Captain Gringo nodded and said, "Okay, but take it easy in that sun. See if you can find any sea turtle eggs while you're at it. Remember the time we dug up those turtle eggs over on the mainland?"

"*Oui*, with considerable disgust. But I have never really shared your New England taste for clams, either."

Gaston left and Captain Gringo went on trying to rub something like heat into the dry palm frond across his bare knees. He had a good groove now, and when he touched it with his finger, it felt warm. But it didn't look like this was the right way to start a fire. Maybe if he improvised a little fire bow, like the Apaches used . . .

Gaston ran back, shouting, "We are saved! There's a sail on the horizon!" So Captain Gringo tossed aside the stubborn wood and went out to join Gaston as the little Frenchman capered up and down, waving the undershirt he'd pulled off at a tea colored lateen sail out to sea. The taller Captain Gringo followed suit. But at first it looked like the crew of whatever it was out there didn't see them. Then the vessel tacked and Gaston chortled, "They see us! They are swinging to rescue us!"

Captain Gringo lowered the undershirt he'd been waving as he frowned seaward. He could see, now, it was a sort of whaleboat-sized craft of unpainted mahogany. The sail was matting, rigged on a bamboo mast and crossboom. The half dozen men in the primitive vessel looked pretty primitive, too. They were almost the same color as the mahogany of their hull and stark naked to boot. "Gaston, you were kidding about Caribs, weren't you?" Gringo asked.

"I thought I was," Gaston answered, "Very few of the sea-going cannibals are said to be left. But there are limits to where the gunboats of our more-advanced civilization may go. Whoever they are, they are obviously Indians."

As the little sailing vessel came closer there was no doubt about it. But most of the tribes along the Mosquito Coast which were still primitive were said to be reasonably friendly, so what the hell.

The boat put in down the beach a ways and the two soldiers of fortune saw, as the Indians beached with methodical movements, that they were acting as if they hadn't noticed two white men waving undershirts at them for the past quarter hour or so. That didn't mean much either way. Indians were like that. They wouldn't have landed on an otherwise worthless key if they'd seen no reason to.

With Gaston trailing, Captain Gringo walked toward the Indians as they hauled their vessel up on the coral sand. They'd lowered the matting lateen and he could now see the boat was little more than a big dugout with extra planking added to the sides to offer sea-keeping freeboard. They were still pretending not to notice him. So he stopped about fifty feet from them and waited, politely. He could hear them talking, or growling, now. It was no language he'd ever heard before, so he knew they weren't from San Blas, which was sort of a shame. He got along pretty well with San Blas Indians.

The strange Indians wore nothing but cords around their bellies and were armed with spears, save for an older stocky guy who packed a trade machete and seemed to be in charge. As the two white men watched at a polite distance, the chief said something and a couple of the others moved over to the tree line to start gathering fire wood, still not looking their way.

18

Another squatted on his haunches, took flint and steel from a pouch attached to his waist cord, and started striking sparks at a handful of dry timber that came with the kit. Captain Gringo muttered, "So that's how you do it. Do you have any idea what's going on, Gaston?"

"I hope not," Gaston replied. "Most obviously they are going to build a fire and, as you said, it is *très* hot on this beach at the moment. So they must intend to cook something, or somebody, non?"

"You think they could be Caribs, then?"

"I don't know. The few Caribs I have seen in my time were either running away or running at me. At such a time one does not study fine details of tribal costume. Shall we try some Creole jargon on them, Dick?"

"Not yet. They see us standing here. If their manners are at all like Apaches, they may wait until they're ready to eat before they notice us and invite us to join them."

"Really? I didn't know you dined that much with Apache when you served with the Tenth Cavalry back in your own country."

"We mostly swapped shots. But some bands were friendly."

"You call that sullen attitude friendly, my old and rare Indian expert?"

"You do if you're an Indian. Just stay cool, damn it. If they weren't figuring on inviting us to lunch, they'd have thrown one of those spears at us by now, see?"

The Indians who'd gathered firewood along the tree line piled dry fronds atop the smoldering tinder and for a time the whole bunch seemed intent on getting the fire going good as they ignored the white men standing only a few yards away. Then the stocky old guy with the machete straightened up, seemed to notice them for the first time, and pointed at them, casually, with the tip of his machete. One of the younger spear packers nodded and, stepped a few paces their way as Captain Gringo called out softly in Spanish to him. The Indian nodded, grinned, and threw his spear straight at Captain Gringo as hard as he could!

19

It missed by a whisker as Captain Gringo side stepped and warned Gaston. "Don't run! You'll get a spear in your back!" He, in turn, started walking backward away from them, now that he knew who they meant to have for lunch indeed!

One of the other red cannibals, grinning boyishly, made what appeared to be a sneering remark about his comrade's aim as he wound up and threw his own spear. But since the white target hadn't panicked and turned his head away, Captain Gringo managed to dodge that one, too. The Indians seemed to find all this very interesting. So, as the two men walked away from them backward, the whole bunch followed, walking, not running, as if they had all the time in the world.

When one considered the odds, and the size of the island, one could see how they might assume they had!

Behind Captain Gringo, Gaston said, conversationally, "You are walking into one of the spears, Dick. I have the other. What's the form?"

Captain Gringo side stepped, risked a quick glance, and snatched the spear stuck in the sand by its hardwood shaft as he replied, "Don't throw. See if we can make the trees where we have a chance for some bayonet stuff."

"Ah, *oui,* they have us at throwing these things in the open. But those trees are *très* far, and they seem to be taking this game seriously!"

"Not yet. They're still enjoying the cat-and-mouse bullshit. I can't see you without turning my head. Are you close enough for some buddy bayonet work?"

"But of course. Did you imagine I wished to take on three-to-one all by myself? Tell me if anyone throws while I have a quick look and, *voila*! We are almost to the trees."

The Indians noticed that, too. One of them wound up to throw his spear. The chief barked at him and he didn't. The fat bastard with the machete knew his business, too, it seemed. The two who'd lost their spears had produced knives from somewhere, but they were out of the picture for the moment as long as the two white men had the longer weapons. The guy with the machete would hang out of spear thrust range, too, now that he was on to their game. So it was two spears to each of theirs, and now leaves were brushing Captain Gringo's bare back. As he crawfished into the palmettos one of the spearmen in the lead yelled something that sounded like "son-of-a-bitch" in any lingo and charged forward at a run, holding his spear at port arms as he saw his intended meal vanish amid the greenery.

He was easy. Captain Gringo was waiting just inside the tree line and as the Carib busted through he ran right into the spear tip braced like a bayoneted rifle against the heavier American's right hip.

The trouble with using a spear as a bayonet was that there was no cross guard or gun muzzle to regulate the depth of the thrust. So the screaming Carib slid his chest along the shaft all the way to Captain Gringo's left fist before he fell sideways, carrying the tip down and exposing the American to the next guy coming through with blood in his eye and another spear in his brown paws. Gaston snapped, "Down!" and as Captain Gringo dropped to his knees atop the man he'd nailed, the Frenchman parried the Indian's spear with his own, stabbed him in the throat with a practiced twist and pitchforked him the other way. Then Captain Gringo put a naked heel in his own victim's face to pull the spear out with a long sucking sound as yet another Indian popped through the leaves at him in time to take the blood-slicked spear in the groin!

Nobody else seemed interested. So Captain Gringo yelled, "After them! Don't let them beat us to that boat!" And, suiting actions to words, he leaped to his feet and charged back the way they'd just retreated.

As he and Gaston broke cover, they saw that only one of the Caribs still had a spear. He and the three others were running back toward their boat as if their lives depended on it, as indeed they did. The only one still able to face Captain Gringo spear-to-spear somehow didn't seem to feel up to it as he ran in a blind funk after the chief with the machete and the two who'd lost their serious weaponry. So as the longer legged American caught up, he speared the Carib in the back, just under the floating ribs, and leaped over his falling body as the old guy with the machete turned and called out in Spanish, *"Por favor, señor!* I am not an evil person! I am a Christian like yourself!"

Then he saw the look in Captain Gringo's eyes and raised his machete to defend himself, a little too late. Grinning wolfishly, the bigger American parried the machete blade with a vertical butt stroke, then reversed his weapon to slice the steel tip down the fat Indian's paunch, spilling his guts and his life on the hot sand, as the two, armed only with knives, passed the beached boat and kept running as fast as they could. As Captain Gringo bent over to pick up the machete, Gaston tore past. Captain Gringo yelled, "Let 'em go. We've got the boat!"

Gaston staggered to a walk, turned with a grin, and said, "Spoilsport. You really need some bayonet practice, Dick. No legionnaire would have hung his blade up like you did back there. The idea is to twist as you thrust, and only go in far enough to kill the bastards, hein?"

"I'll keep that in mind. Let's launch the boat before those other guys circle around and pick up those spears their buddies dropped."

Gaston agreed that was a neat idea, so they both put their backs into it. And though six men had dragged the boat ashore, the two of them soon had the Indian craft afloat in the shallows and climbed in. Gaston asked, "Do you know how to sail a lateen rig?" and Captain Gringo replied, "We'll learn. Let's just use these paddles and get out to sea a ways before we experiment."

With each of them paddling on one side, this was soon accomplished. As they looked back, the two Carib who'd run away were shouting terrible things at them on shore as they waved spears in futile rage. Captain Gringo laughed and said, "See what I mean? I hope the bastards enjoy that island as much as we did. Let's take stock and see what's in those baskets between us. I hope at least they had some sea rations aboard."

They hadn't. As the two soldiers of fortune explored the meager belongings of their would-be attackers, they found nothing but some clothing one could assume the Indians had taken from some white or mestizo settlers they'd raided along the Mosquito Coast.

Gaston put on a straw peon hat and observed, "I thought they seemed rather hungry. There's a few grains of parched corn here. I would assume they were running low on provisions when they saw us on shore and decided to have us for lunch. Ah, here is a pair of white twill pants close to my size. At least we shall arrive on shore properly dressed, non?"

"Screw the duds. See any guns or, better yet, drinking water?"

Gaston rummaged around on his side of the pile and held up a gourd, saying, "This seems to be water. No guns. One hardly expects to be attacked by spears when anyone has guns, non? The poor peons they robbed these pathetic belongings from no doubt were weaponless, too, at the time. One seldom meets truculent cannibal Indians when one is armed. That must be why we hear so little of them these days, hein? Here is a shirt about your size, Dick, and, wonder of wonders, what is this in the breast pocket? A cigar! Not only a cigar, but a Havana Perfecto! The previous owner of this outfit must have been returning from town when they jumped him."

Captain Gringo took the peon shirt and put it on. It was tight, but it beat sunburn. He found a straw hat, put it on, and was rummaging for something that might pass for pants when Gaston sighed and said, "This is all too cruel to bear! The stuff in this gourd is really only water and I can't find a single *match* amid all this loot!"

Captain Gringo found a pair of white twill drawers and pulled them on, gingerly. They were tight as hell, but if he didn't bend over they might not split for a while. "How's that for Robinson Crusoe, Gaston?" he laughed. "We started out with nothing and now we're all dressed up with somewhere to go, if I can get this sail to work."

He told Gaston to move aft and take the tiller as he gingerly stepped the bamboo mast and started to hoist the lateen sail. He knew how to sail a fore-and-aft rig, but the funny triangular lateen looked tricky. He wet a finger, said, "Hell, the wind is from the east and we want to go west, so I'll run her up as a square sail and we'll try her the easy way."

As he hoisted the unfamiliar clumsy sail, the trade wind billowed it open and they began to move across the swells toward the afternoon sun at a modest clip. But Gaston, still bitching as Captain Gringo sat down to enjoy the ride, muttered, "*Sacre Dieu,* I am dying for a smoke. I possess a perfectly good cigar, and I have no triple-titted matches! Is there no justice under this species of tropic sun?"

Captain Gringo squinted past Gaston at the far horizon and asked, in a morose tone, "Do you think I can pass for a peon in this outfit, Gaston?"

"*Merde alors,* don't speak to me of such mundane matters when I need a light! My problem is *très* serious, Dick!"

"So is mine. No shit, do you think I could be taken for a native in this straw hat and white cotton twill?"

"Don't be ridiculous. If you didn't have an American accent and were dressed like a gentleman, you might possibly pass for a Castilian. But most of the people who dress like peons in this part of the world tend to be small and dark. What difference does it make? I already know who you are and there is nobody else for miles, right?"

"Wrong. Take a gander off to the south."

Gaston turned, stared a moment at the vessel coming over the horizon with a bone in it's teeth and said, "I stand corrected. Off hand, I would say a gunboat is

24

headed our way. Can you make out her colors with your young and virile eyes, my peon lad?"

"Yeah, she's Guatemalan, flying a navy insignia, and if she hasn't seen us I can't figure any other reason for her to be headed our way, can you?"

It was becoming fashionable for high brows to sneer at the "Gunboat Diplomacy" of the late Victorian era. But there was no getting around the fact that it worked. When an armor-plated tub, packing four pounders, hoves into view, anyone from a piss-pot dictator to two guys in a sailboat tended to listen politely to what you had to say. So when the gunboat bearing down on them signaled Captain Gringo and Gaston to heave to, they dropped the sail and did so.

The lettering on the craft's steel bow said she was the *Matador,* which sounded Guatemalan enough. But they saw she was a Clyde-built steamram, pretty modern for a bush league navy flying the colors of a banana republic. A couple of guys in spiffy white uniforms were waiting at the top of the ship's ladder as one of the crewmen threw them a line. The two soldiers of fortune had had time to whip up a cover story that skated close enough to the truth to give them a sporting chance. So after making fast to the ladder, they climbed aboard. Gaston had suggested he do the talking. After wandering around these parts since deserting the Legion in Mexico a generation ago, Gaston's Spanish was better than his English and he could pass for a native if he had to. And right now he had to. They both knew the authorities of too many countries to mention, including Guatemala, were looking for a tall blond American in his early thirties and a short middle-aged Frenchman. On the other hand, that unexpected shipwreck could cover a multitude of sins, like not having proper identification, right?

As they reached the deck, Gaston smiled at the pink-faced dandy with the ranking stripes on his tropic whites and said, in Spanish, "You have no idea how pleased we are to have been found, Lieutenant! I am called Carlos Garcia y Maldonado. This other caballero is Señor Martin, a Canadian, I believe. We were shipwrecked together but, alas, he does not speak much Spanish, so I know little about him."

Captain Gringo thought it was a pretty nifty snow job, too. If they didn't know each other well, they could hardly be those two guys travelling together. And if he wasn't supposed to speak much Spanish, they couldn't question him too much.

Then the skipper of the gunboat turned to him and asked, in ever so veddy veddy English, "British subject, are you? I say, this is a spot of luck! I *understand* the lingo of these perishing Dons, but it makes one feel foolish trying to *speak* it! I do hope you have an explanation for what you two were doing aboard that pirate craft, Martin. Hate to have to put a fellow white man in irons and all that."

Captain Gringo frowned and bought some time to think by saying, "I'm surprised to find a British officer in command of a Guatemalan gunboat, ah, Lieutenant . . . ?"

"Webster, rowed for Harrow. You find British officers in command because Whitehall, for some odd reason, seems to think our client state needs a navy, and we could hardly have Guatemalans running a modern warship, eh what? We were discussing your boarding us from that pirate's longboat, Old Chum. Must say it came as a surprise to find two white men manning her. The last we heard, she was crewed by raiding Caribs."

Captain Gringo said, "She was. Señor Garcia and I stole her from some Indians who landed on the key we

27

were marooned on. You see, we were aboard the Honduran schooner, *Serpiente,* when she was run down by a steam freighter in the fog."

"British Honduran or Honduras Honduran?" Webster cut in, adding, "Such a bother, having two bloody countries with the same name, what?"

Captain Gringo nodded and replied, "I think the *Serpiente* was from the one that speaks Spanish. Anyway, this other gent and me wound up in the water and lost everything but our underwear. We made it to a key you'll find just over the horizon to the east if you want to hang the two Caribs we left stranded there when we grabbed their boat."

The dapper Englishman thought, which seemed to strain him terribly, then shrugged a reply, "Can't see them bothering anyone marooned on a perishing key with the hurricane season coming on. We captured the ruddy pirate craft, and that was our mission, eh what? You two can come along with us to Puerto Barrios and sort it out with the civilian authorities there. I fear conditions aboard *Matador* are a bit cramped, but we'll try to make you comfortable, eh what?"

"That's very kind of you, Lieutenant, but we were headed for Costa Rica, if you don't mind."

"Mind? Why should I mind? Go anywhere you like, once your respective consulates in Puerto Barrios issue you new passports. I can see it's a bit out of your way and all that, but *Matador* is a steamram, not a bloody taxi boat. They'll want to know about the collision at sea, too. I don't mean to sound suspicious—one can see you're both gentlemen and all that. But I must say I find it odd that the steamer who ran you down didn't stop to pick up survivors. Rules of the sea, you know."

Captain Gringo nodded, and bitterly said, "We found it pretty odd, too. The sons-of-bitches just steamed on and left us in the drink to drown."

Webster frowned and said, "Oh, I say, that wasn't very nice of them. Even in fog, one would think they'd have noticed hitting another vessel, and not seraching for survivors simply isn't done. Must have been one of these eccentric Latin skippers, eh what? No offense Señor Garcia, here, but it was rather well established back in the days of Good Queen Bess that Spanish types just didn't have the knack at sea."

Gaston, who was pretending to be a Spaniard, naturally protested, in his fake Castilian, "That well may be your Anglo-Saxon opinion, Señor, but the ship that ran us down and left us to our fate was British! She was the *S.S. Imperial Trader,* out of Liverpool. She was close enough for us to make out her name in the fog. But she did not stop for us, as you can see!"

Captain Gringo could have kicked him.

Webster blinked in astonishment and gasped, "The *Imperial Trader?* I find this astonishing! I know the *Imperial Trader*. She belongs to an old and respected trading company, running between Blighty and the crown colony of British Honduras! Forget her skipper's name, but I know him on sight, ashore. You gentlcmcn have made a very serious charge against a master sailing under the British merchant ensign! I do hope your business in Costa Rica wasn't pressing. Don't see how you'll be able to leave until you testify at the board of inquiry, now!"

The two castaways were quartered in a tiny cabin with upper and lower bunks, and issued shoes and a pair of white duck pants that fit Captain Gringo. They were not issued guns to replace the ones they'd lost, of course, and while they didn't seem to be under guard, there was nowhere to go if they wanted to make a break for it.

They didn't just want to make a break for it. They *had* to make a break for it before the damned *Matador* delivered them into the hands of the civilian authorities in Puerto Barrios! The skipper and crew of the steamram seemed willing to take their tale at face value, unless Webster was one of those Iron Fist in the Velvet Glove types. You never knew with Englishmen of his class. The sun never set on the British Empire these days because, despite their twittery manners, some tended to be tough, ruthless, and smarter than they let on. But whether Webster suspected anything or not, the Guatemalan government probably had a hard-on for one Richard Walker, a.k.a. Captain Gringo, and couldn't be too happy about Legion Deserter Gaston Verrier, either, after that little border incident a few weeks back. Even if they didn't know about their short hitch in an enemy state's army, every police station in Latin America was plastered with reward posters and very good likenesses of Captain Gringo, at least. How could he have known when he'd sat for those U.S. Army I.D. photos in his misspent youth, that someday they'd be haunting him from so many walls?

The seventy-two hour voyage was uneventful, which is to say that try as they might, neither of them could come up with anything better in the way of ideas than jumping overboard. And while that would certainly save them a lot of questions in Puerto Barrios, Webster kept *Matador* well out to sea in shark infested waters, so there had to be a better way.

Captain Gringo clung to the hope they might steam into the Guatemalan seaport after sunset. A last-minute swim under cover of darkness beat trying to bluff his way past the Canadian consulate as a non-existent Canadian who'd be checked out by cablegram in no time at all. But, again, the British skipper belied his dithery appearance by timing it so that they arrived early in the morning so that he wouldn't have to guide his vessel into dubiously charted shiplanes in the dark. Mercifully, *Matador* was not one of the few vessels now equipped with the new Marconi wireless telegraph, so at least the authorities ashore wouldn't be expecting them. If Webster kept things casual, they might be allowed to walk down the gang plank unescorted and do some side street ducking after telling him they sure were in a hurry to get to their respective consulates.

But, again, the British skipper turned out to be smarter, or more suspicious, than he let on. As Gringo and Gaston came out on deck to await the landing, a junior officer walked aft to them, leading a quartet of Royal Marines. He said, "Lieutenant Webster's compliments, gentlemen. He regrets he can't leave the bridge at the moment. But I've been ordered to escort you safely to the Canadian and Costa Rican consulates."

"With Royal Marines?" Captain Gringo asked in a desperately casual voice. The J.G. nodded and said,

"Yessir. Crowded unruly port and all that. Wouldn't want anything to happen to you before we saw you safely to the civilian authorities."

The tall American shot Gaston a look. Gaston shrugged. They'd fought side-by-side often long enough to know what the other was thinking. Gaston didn't see what they could do, either. Leaving aside the fact that the marines were tougher and more highly trained than average soldiers in these parts, and packing repeating rifles, neither of the soldiers of fortune knew Puerto Barrios. So even if they made a break on shore, where in the hell could they run?

Captain Gringo stared morosely at the waterfront they were approaching. Puerto Barrios lay on a peninsula jutting out from the mainland of Guatemala, so it faced west with the trade winds blowing over its right shoulder. It didn't look like a big town. The stucco buildings looming behind the waterfront were Spanish Baroque and most of them were painted various shades of pink, from dusky rose to baby's asshole. That was partly because of the local love of color and partly to save the eyes of anyone forced to look at all that stucco under a blinding tropic sun. At this latitude, plain white stucco glared at noon like the arc of a welder's torch. He couldn't tell if the hazy blur of blue green above the tiled roof tops were hills behind the town or the tops of massive jungle trees. Either meant a place to hide, if they could get to them. But getting to them wasn't going to be easy. There didn't seem to be much town, so there wouldn't be much in the way of alleyways. Would these Royal Marines risk firing at them on a street crowded with dusky peon types? Yeah, they would. People packing guns in Her Majesty's Service didn't worry much about ruddy natives with dark complexions.

The J.G. was prattling away, not saying anything important but trying to be polite, as the *Matador* steamed dead slow toward a landing quay. Captain Gringo didn't have to be told that they were about to land—he could

32

see! He asked the J.G. if he spoke Spanish. The young Englishman blinked in confusion and replied, "Hardly. Why on Earth should I?"

"Oh, I dunno. Thought that since you were serving aboard a gunboat flying Guatemalan colors, you might have picked some up?"

The J.G. laughed, "Not bloody likely. We usually spend shore leaves in British Honduras, where even the niggers speak proper English. Don't worry when we go ashore, though. The natives here know enough to get out of a white man's way."

Captain Gringo nodded thoughtfully at the marine and said, "Yeah, I should think they would. I know this is none of my business, but how come this vessel has an Hispanic name and sails under a Latin American flag if it's part of the Royal Navy?"

The J.G. frowned and said, "I'll be dashed if I know. Something to do with bloody Yanks and their bloody *Monroe Doctrine,* I suppose. You see, Guatemala's not part of the Empire, exactly, but we regard her as a client state."

"Yeah, I heard about the Bank Of England funding the Guatemalan national debt a while back. Naturally, you guys will be in better shape to collect if you take the trouble of running the Guatemalan armed forces off their local government's hands, huh?"

The J.G. smiled and replied, "I see you do understand the rather exciting politics in this part of the world. This nasty little seaport is named for the late dictator, General Barrios, who managed to leave his country in a dreadful mess when he was killed invading El Salvador a while back, for reasons that elude sensible historians. The Bank Of England did indeed save the odd little land from drowning in a sea of debts, to save the British investments here. The loan was granted to the current junta, led by some blighter called Cabrera, who took over when General Barrios' nephew and El Presidente were assassinated. Naturally, another faction led by some Don called Barillas

33

keeps trying to overthrow Cabrera, and we can't have that, can we?"

"Not until the dictator you're backing pays off the loan. Meanwhile, since he is a dictator, and Guatemala has this unfortunate habit of starting wars all over the place, you don't want Cabrera in a position to invade any of his neighbors without Her Majesty's permission, right?"

"Exactly. That's why I haven't tried to learn the lingo. Ruddy political situation is complicated enough. I say, they're putting the gangway down. Shall we toddle you chaps on to your consulates?"

Captain Gringo nodded as if he thought it was a swell idea. As they were escorted to the gangway, Gaston said something to one of the marines in Spanish and got a blank look in return. Good old Gaston. Now they knew none of the guys escorting them, or guarding them, spoke Spanish.

Captain Gringo nodded to the marine and said, in English, "Señor Garcia was asking you how far it was to the Costa Rican consulate." So the marine answered not far, and Captain Gringo pretended to translate as he told Gaston in Spanish, "Good thinking. You keep an eye peeled to the left. I'll cover the right, and when either of us sees an opening, we go for it, agreed?"

Gaston shrugged and said, "All right, but what if we have to split up?" "I'll meet you back in San José. I sure don't mean to hang around here looking for you if I can bust loose."

By this time they were going down the gangway, single file. The J.G. politely allowed the two soldiers of fortune to go ashore first, but sent two marines ahead of them to "clear a passage," the wise-ass bastard!

They were polite, too. So they waited on the quay for him to come ashore with the other marines. He pointed his chin up the nearest street running inland and said, "We'll take you to the Canadian consulate first, Martin."

Gaston said something in Spanish. Captain Gringo

34

nodded and asked, "Couldn't Señor Garcia run on alone to his, to save time?"

"Oh, hardly. Orders and all that."

"Okay, why don't we drop him off first, then? Once you leave me at the Canadian consulate, you'll have no translator. He doesn't speak English and I think he's sort of confused already."

The J.G. shot the small Frenchman a look of dismissal and asked, "How can one tell? They all act confused, even when they know what they're doing. I'm afraid he'll have to wait his turn. You're the British subject, here. He's only a native!"

Captain Gringo turned to "explain" to "the native" as they all started walking in the morning heat. What he really said was, "You got that? They have you down as nobody much. So you'll have the best chance of making a break, when and if."

Gaston replied in Spanish, "I can see that, insulting as it is. But what about you?"

"If you see a chance, grab it! Why let them hang two instead of one? I'll be all right if you get away, for the moment. We're not supposed to know each other and they have you down as an excitable native dim-wit who might do something crazy anyway."

As they left the waterfront, the street was crowded and it was obvious it was a market day. Colorfully dressed women of every complexion jostled one another, laughing, as they picked over the wares and produce on the push carts cluttering the right of way. The J.G. clucked disapprovingly at such uncivilized behavior and two of the marines moved forward to clear the way with their bayoneted rifles. The rifles did the job better than the loud curses they hurled at the natives, in the apparent belief that if one shouted loud enough in English, anyone with a lick of sense would understand you. Captain Gringo felt embarrassed for the J.G. as the crowd gave way, some laughing and others shooting dirty looks. Couldn't he see that this was a pretty stupid way to make friends for his empire? The Brits had built the whole thing in one queen's long lifetime. He didn't see how her grandchildren were going to hang on to it if they didn't show some manners to their darker skinned subjects, and these Guatemalans weren't even British subjects. He wondered how British colonial officers dealt with folks in India and Africa, and how loyal to the Crown it made them all feel.

But the rudeness of the shore party served its purpose, though not the one the J.G. had in mind. Gaston took advantage of it by suddenly diving into the dark slit between two buildings and, as Gaston had foreseen, it took their escort a few vital seconds to notice.

The J.G. gasped, "I say!" as he stared at where Gaston had been walking just a moment ago. Then he yelled, "Peters and Flynn, after the idiot!"

Then, as two of the marines dove into the slot after Gaston with guns at port arms, the J.G. frowned at Captain Gringo and asked, "What on earth made him do that, do you suppose?"

Captain Gringo shrugged and answered, "He didn't say. I told you he was anxious about something."

The crowd, of course, sensed a *situacion* and eagerly closed around them to enjoy whatever it was. In any marketplace in Latin America, a *situacion* was an entertaining event and the grinning peon women wanted to have something new to talk about, so they all started shouting questions and even answers at once. A very fat mestiza shoved between Captain Gringo and the J.G. So the tall American stepped politely back to give her room, and then, since the J.G. wasn't looking at him, he took yet another.

Somewhere in the distance a rifle fired. The marine nearest Captain Gringo gasped, "Blighty!" and at least half the women screamed. He had three more fairly fat ones between him and the marine now, and the marine

36

was trying to catch the J.G.'s eye for further instructions. So Captain Gringo eased around behind a push cart, smiling innocently.

The pushcart had its canvas tarps hanging almost to the ground over the wheels to expose the peppers and papayas on sale. The owner was a dark but probably mostly white girl, wearing flounced red skirts and a low-cut peon blouse anyone with tits like that should have been ashamed of. Her face wasn't bad, either. He didn't want any peppers or papayas, but he smiled at her anyway as he gauged his chances for a dash to that doorway on the far side of the street. She looked him over with her sort of wicked gypsy eyes and said, "That door is locked. Are you trying to get away from those stupid British, Querido?"

Querido meant sweetheart and she'd just told him what she thought of his British escort, so he nodded, cautiously. She said, "Under my cart."

He glanced around, saw nobody was looking his way, and took her suggestion. It was sort of cozy under the pushcart with the canvas hanging down all around, but the canvas ended a good four or five inches off the cobbles and he could see everybody's damned feet.

He heard the J.G. yelling a lot and then a brace of feet wearing the boots of the Royal Marines ran past his makeshift hideout on the double. He heard them pounding on wood. He could see the girl had been right about that big patio door being locked. He couldn't see why she was sticking her pretty neck out for him. But if nobody thought to look under here, she'd obviously just saved his!

A familiar set of feet came over to the cart and stopped. Captain Gringo could have reached out and given the J.G. a hot foot from where he crouched under the pushcart, but he didn't feel like playing any more jokes right now. The J.G. said, "I say, señorita. Did a big blond chap just pass by you?"

She answered, "No hablo Ingles, señor."

"Oh, drat. You look rather intelligent, too. Listen, big hombre! Mucho blondo! Which way did he go?"

"Por favor, no comprendo, cabron Ingles."

"Goddamn it, girl. Listen to me. Ah . . . hombre grande. Going like so with his feet, see?"

Captain Gringo bit a knuckle to keep from laughing outloud as the J.G. ran in place. The pushcart girl above him said, "Tu madre! No comprendo, hijo de puta Ingles" in a bored tone. Captain Gringo could see her ankles, and they were nice indeed, but he felt like kicking her. She was breaking him up. She wasn't just acting dumb. She was taking advantage of the language barrier to tell the poor J.G. what she thought of him, and she apparently thought he was a pimp for his wife and the son of a whore!

The pair of boots with a marine in them joined the J.G.'s a few inches from Captain Gringo's sweating nose. It was hot and stuffy under here. The marine said, "We lost him, Sir. Do you suppose they could have been in on it together?"

"Dash it all, Flynn, you can't be that stupid! Of course they were together in whatever in blue blazes it was. The skipper was right. There was more to those blokes than met the eye. And now we've lost both the buggers! I'm going to catch it for this, Flynn, and you-lot know what that means, next shore leave, so don't ask, Goddamn your eyes!"

"What are we to do now, Sir?"

"What *can* we do, dammit? We'll have to go back to *Matador* and let the local police look for the buggers. Even if we spoke Spanish, the Queen's writ doesn't run here in Guatemala. Besides, it's Guatemala's problem, now. Let *them* worry about what it was all about."

The feet walked away. Captain Gringo stayed right where he was until what seemed a million years went by. Then, as he was sure he was about to pass out from the stuffy heat, one corner of the canvas lifted and the girl who'd saved him said, "You can come out now. Just stand up slowly, as if you were looking for something for me under my cart, no?"

He crawled out and gingerly got to his feet. None of the other people in the crowd seemed interested. He smiled down at her and said, "I wish there was some way to thank you, señorita . . . ?"

"I am called Vivaracha. You could buy some of my nice hot peppers, if you like, señor . . . ?"

"Call me Dick. I'd love to buy your hot stuff, Vivaracha, but I have no money."

She sighed in resignation and said, "Ah, just my luck. Those stupid British soldiers robbed you, eh? What did they arrest you for? I hope you took a shot at their nasty old queen, or at least one of her relatives."

He didn't want to go into the whole story. He didn't want her to think he was an assassin, either. So he said. "It was just a mix-up. I had no papers and for some reason that seemed to upset them."

"Ah, yes, governments can be so tedious about papers. Do you have any friends here in Puerto Barrios to hide among, Deek?"

He shook his head and said, "I'm afraid not. I've never been here before. But, thanks to you, at least I have a running start. Could you tell me how far it is to the nearest border, Vivaracha?"

"Too far," she laughed. "Those others will tell our own police about you and our police can be equally tedious about strangers, however handsome, who haven't neither money nor proper identification. It will soon be siesta time and business is very poor today in any case. I think I had better take you home with me, Deek."

"I'd like that very much, Vivaracha, but I told you I have no money."

She looked hurt and answered. "What do you take me for? I sell pepper and papaya. Nothing else. Just for being so cruel, I am going to make you push my cart. But we had better hurry, eh?"

He watched, bemused, as the well-endowed but wirey

39

peon girl flopped the canvas back over her wares and pointed with her pretty chin at the handle bar. As a matter of fact, she looked like a gal who sold more than pepper and papaya, and she was coming on mighty bold for an Hispanic girl, too. But what did he have to lose? He'd already told her he didn't have a damned thing on him. He felt naked without his gun as he hefted the cart handle and started rolling it as directed. She walked at his side. He kept his head down, like the cart was heavier than it was. In these ragged clothes and straw hat, he might pass, at a casual glance, for a rather large peon trundling unsold wares from the market place. It beat just running, until he had some notion where in Hell to run to!

Vivaracha steered him down a narrow side street, then up an alley to where she lived. It appeared to be a converted carriage house off the alley behind a bigger house. As he commented, she explained he was right. This part of town had once been grander. The hidalgos who'd built the layout had moved to the more fashionable part of town and the main house was now a courtyard tenement inhabited by pobrecitos, like herself. She opened the big door of the erstwhile carriage house and he ran the cart inside. He assumed, like most Latins, she lived with an extended clan. So he was braced for all the introductions and explanations before they got around to feeding him or sending for the cops, depending.

But when Vivaracha led him through a curtained archway into her main quarters, he saw there was nobody else there. She had three quarters of the old building sparsely furnished for Hidalgo tastes, but pretty spiffy for a pushcart lady.

There was a beehive corner fireplace with a cooking hearth and a big four-poster with mosquito netting in another corner. Big oak chests sat against the stucco walls and the walls were the exact pink one associates with the nipples of a virgin. He warned himself not to think about the pink walls like that. Vivaracha didn't look like a virgin and he'd told her he had no money. Just why in hell she'd brought him home eluded him, but it was her place, so it was dealer's choice.

Vivaracha sat him down by the cold fireplace and moved over to the windows to shut the blinds as she said, "Bueno, it will soon be La Siesta. If the police can bestir themselves to look for anybody at such a time, the streets will be empty, they will quickly dash back to tell everyone you are not in Puerto Barrios as they cool off in the shade, no?"

"I hope you're right, Vivaracha. What's to stop them from assuming I'm inside with someone, like I am?"

She shrugged and said, "What else *can* they assume, once they see you are not in any public place? On the other hand, where would you start looking if you were a tired policeman? There are many houses here, and there is no reason for them to connect a desperado off a British gunboat with a respectable street peddler who has no recorded political views, eh?"

"That makes sense. What are your political views, Vivaracha?"

She parted the mosquito netting to sit on the bed, lifting one knee to remove a sandal as she replied, "I'm against the present government, of course. That's why I helped you get away from those Englishmen. All true Guatemalans hate the English."

He didn't know how to take what she was doing with her sandals. Maybe her feet hurt? Anything else was too much to hope for! So he kept his voice casual as he asked, "How come? I heard the Bank Of England just saved Guatemala with a big loan."

She looked disgusted and said, "The Cabrera junta should be ashamed of themselves for *taking* it! Do you think the British offered because they admire our big blue eyes? As long as we are in debt to England, our so-called government cannot object to the way they are looting our country! Do you know what a single mahogany log is

41

worth, Deek? More than a working man in this country will see in years! Those estupidos in Guatemala City have agreed to let English companies cut our standing mahogany, por nada, not even taxes. Not even paying for the damages they do to our land!"

"Well, you have to admit there must be a lot of trees out there in your rain forest, right?"

"Wrong!" she snapped, explaining, "It takes a hundred years for a mahogany tree to grow large enough to cut. And the trees do not grow in rows, like your pines. The mahogany grows scattered through the forest, mixed with other timber, like rubber, chicle, balsa, and less valuable trees. These English pigs only wish to cut mahogany. But when they go into our forests they cut down everything, to clear their path. The damage is terrible. After the loggers have passed through, the sun bakes the red soil to what looks like terra cotta tile. Nothing will ever grow on it again. They cut near the village I was born in, two years ago. Nobody lives there now. It's a desert of hard red clay. The heat and drifting red dust kills crops for kilometers around."

He nodded and said something agreeable as he tried to size her up. Vivaracha sure didn't look like a person who was interested in tropical botany. As a matter of fact, she seemed to be taking her clothes off!

She tossed her blouse over the back of a bedside chair, exposing a heroic pair of breasts with nipples a lot darker indeed than her stucco walls. As she went to work on the fasteners of her red flounce skirts, she saw he was just sitting there and asked, "Don't you wish to take off your own clothes, Deek? I feel embarrassed undressing all by myself."

He put his straw hat carefully on the nearby hearth and stood up to start unbuttoning his shirt as he said, smiling, "I didn't know I was invited, but as long as it's siesta time . . . "

"Sí, it will be better if anyone who might come by were to find you in bed, where all honest men belong during

La Siesta. I do not think anyone will, but we cannot afford to take chances."

Then she turned around, dropped the skirts to expose a firm pair of buttocks that matched her breasts just right, and popped into bed before he'd had time to examine her for distinguishing marks.

The nice thing about low-cut shoes was that you just had to kick them off, and the nice thing about having nothing in your pockets was that you could just let the damned pants fall anywhere they wanted to. So he stepped out of them and joined her in the four-poster.

She had her naked back turned to him as he lifted the covers and slid in. But when he reached out to take her in his arms, she stiffened and asked, "What are you doing? I told you I was not that kind of woman, Deek!"

He muttered, "Aw, shit," in English, and let go, rolling on his back to stare up at the bed canopy with an annoyed frown. She lay quietly a few moments. Then, still not looking his way, she said, in a martyred tone of understanding, "I suppose you may have gotten the wrong idea about me when I suggested we get into bed for to look innocent, no?"

He growled, "Something like that. I've heard of bundling with everybody fully dressed, but this'll be the first time I've tried it stark naked."

"Are you angry with me, Deek?"

"Hey, what's to be angry about? I owe you for what you did in the marketplace back there, so if you want to play games, I'll let you play games. Go to sleep if you want. I won't make that mistake again."

She didn't answer for a long time. He wondered if she was asleep. He didn't ask. He knew he wasn't going to sleep, so it figured to be a long tedious siesta indeed.

He tried to keep his mind from dwelling on the desirable female next to him by dwelling on the cops that had to be combing every back alley for him and Gaston by now. But he knew Vivaracha was right about them having no reason to look for him here, and he hadn't had a woman for a long time. He knew he could control his hands, but his damned old organ grinder was stiff as a tent pole under the sheets.

Vivaracha sniffed and said, with her face turned to the pink stucco wall, "Well?" So he asked, "Well what?"

"I have been waiting for you to demand an explanation. Now that I have had time to consider, I can see you might think I am teasing you."

He laughed sardonically and said, "Querida, I've been teased by experts. You said you wanted to keep this platonic, so if that's what you want, that's what we'll do. Go to sleep, damn it."

"I'm not sleepy. Don't you find me desirable, Deek?"

"Of course I do. But let's not play kid games. Neither one of us is a kid."

"If I told you I was a virgin," she giggled, "would you believe me?"

He snorted in disgust and answered, "No, but I fail to see what possible difference that could make. If you don't want to make love, I won't make love to you. I never ask for explanations, Vivaracha. I don't sit up and beg, either."

She rolled over, propping herself up on one elbow as she regarded him thoughtfully, her one breast dangling by his face. She asked, "You are not like other men, Deek."

"Yeah, that's what they keep telling me at the office. What were you expecting, a wrestling match?"

"Well, I'm not the sort of woman who can just give herself to a man like a wayward puta."

"I noticed. I'm not going to put us through one of those half-baked semi-rape scenes, Vivaracha. If you want to make love, move a little closer and we'll start all over. If you don't, let's just forget it."

She frowned like a kid who'd fallen off her roller skates and couldn't understand how she'd done a dumb thing like that. She coyly started to lift the sheet to see how she was doing. He started to roll away to keep her from seeing his enraged erection. But then, it wasn't his fault he had one,

44

so he stayed put until she took a peek, gasped, *"Madre de Dios*!" and blushed beet red.

He said, "I hope you're satisfied." And she threw herself atop him to blurt, "You *know* I am not satisfied, you brute!"

So he kissed her, rolled her over on her back, and proceeded to treat her in a more grown-up way. But as he eased into the saddle between her soft tawny thighs, Vivaracha bit her lip, tried to close her legs, and gasped, "No, wait, I don't think I can!"

And then her eyes opened wide as he slid into her and she sighed, "Oh, it seems I can, after all! But be gentle with me, Deek. You are very large, in every way, and I am not used to this with any man."

Then her hips made a liar of her as she braced a naked heel against the mattress on either side of him and proceeded to bump and grind like a pro on her night off with a lover she was very fond of.

She was a great lay and he sure needed it, but even as he started pounding her to glory, Captain Gringo wondered, with one small part of his fugitive's mind, just what the hell was going on here.

The place was maybe a little tacky by North American standards, but he couldn't fathom how a pushcart gal could afford such a fancy spread by the standards down here. She said she only sold hot peppers. He could tell from the hot stuff she was serving up to him right now that if she sold *that* on the side it would more than account for her nicely furnished little pink place. She dug her nails into his back as she started to move her other little place madly. He couldn't tell if she was faking it when she proclaimed her climax. But after having been so long without even an ugly woman, Captain Gringo fired off a charge that almost bounced him off her beautiful body by the recoil.

As they collapsed in each other's arms, Vivaracha crooned, "Have I pleased you, Querido?"

She certainly had and he said so. But the last broad

he'd heard that from had been a border-town whore working for a bigger tip than usual. Captain Gringo wasn't too experienced with pure professionals, thanks to having too romantic a nature to pay if he could get it any other way. But like other Victorian lads of his generation, he'd been to a few parlor houses in his teens, and if this wasn't a professional set up, he hadn't been paying attention back in his horny cadet days at West Point.

But what the hell was she up to, if she was a pro? He'd already told her he had no dinero, damn it!

Sure he had. And she'd said, at first, that she didn't want to lay him. Had the game been, "I'm not that kind of girl, so force me" or had it been, "Now that I've got you down to the wire, make me a cash offer."

She moved her hips teasingly and said if he was tired she'd get on top. So he rolled off her and on to his back to let her. Since he really didn't have a penny, it didn't matter what her game was and, damn, she had a nice little twat!

Vivaracha forked a slim tawny thigh across him and settled down on the tip of his erection to slowly sink into his lap with a moan of pleasure. He moaned, too, for in this position, as she'd no doubt forseen, he was even deeper into her velvety vagina. She braced her palms against his chest with her oversized breasts squeezed between her locked upper arms, and began to ride him like a wicked child on a slow merry-go-round, milking his shaft with long teasing strokes while he admired the view. She'd closed the shutters but spangles of sunlight lanced through the round holes drilled in the oak shutters for ventilation and gave her lithe feline body reversed leopard spots that shifted over her dark flesh as she moved. He put a hand on each of her breasts to play with her swollen nipples. That made him hotter and she smiled down, eyes slitted with her own erotic pleasure as she felt him growing like Jack's beanstalk inside her. But her slow slithering movements were driving him nuts. So he slid his palms down her flanks to cup her buttocks in each hand and help her bounce a little faster. She gritted her teeth and gasped, "Oh, it's starting to hurt in this position, now that I've raised you properly!"

He'd noticed her dimensions were small and it was distracting to him to hit bottom with every stroke, too. So he rolled her over to finish old-fashion again, and this time it was even better. Vivaracha had gotten over her first shyness and was ready to lay him like an old friend. So they let themselves go and, naturally, it took a little longer to get there and the resultant orgasm was protracted and even more sensual.

Captain Gringo knew he was usually good for three orgasms in a row with any reasonably good partner and Vivaracha was prettier and tighter than a lot of ladies he'd met in his time. But as he started moving again, she murmured, "Wait, let's rest a moment, Querido. We have the whole siesta ahead of us, no?"

He rolled out of her love-saddle, nestled her head on his shoulder with her long black hair spread across his heaving chest, and said, "I could use a breather and smoke, if I hadn't left all my cigars and matches on the bottom of the sea."

"Do you wish for me to run out and buy some tobacco, Querido?"

"Don't be silly. I told you I didn't have any money, and where could you buy cigars during the siesta in any case?"

She lay there thinking in his arms as she fondled him for a time. Then she asked, "*Es verdad*? You really have no money at all? I thought perhaps you were saying that because you thought I was a wicked woman who asked for men to pay."

The thought had crossed his mind, but all he answered was, "You can go through my pockets if you want. I told you I was in a shipwreck. I don't even really own the hat and clothes, if you want to get technical."

"*Ay, Querido pobrecito*! How far did you expect to get with no dinero in this cruel uncaring world?"

He answered by running his free hand down her smooth belly as he chuckled, "Well, I've gotten farther than I expected, considering."

But as his fingers forked through the thatch between her thighs, she protested, "Wait. I wish to do it right the next time."

"We've been doing it wrong?"

"We've been doing it lovely. But I, too, enjoy to smoke as we rest and calm our flesh between times. Let me go. I can dress like a flash and be back in moments with cigars for you and cigarettes for me. Maybe I can get us something to drink, too."

"Jesus, you sure are a perfect hostess, Vivaracha, but it's still La Siesta. Nothing will be open."

"Not true, Querido. It's a myth that life comes to a complete standstill during La Siesta. There are always emergencies such as ours, and there is always a greedy shopkeeper who stays open. I know a hacienda, over on the next street, where one can purchase dire necessities by way of a side door though they are officially closed. Do not be proud about having no money. I come from a poor family and have been pennyless more than once, so I know the feeling. Rest your big beautiful body while I run and get refreshments, eh?"

"I don't know, Vivaracha. I've never sponged off a woman before. It makes me feel like a damned pimp."

She took his wrist and slid his questing hand over her mons as she laughed and said, "Don't speak foolishly. A pimp is a man who sells this to others, no? Never fear, I'm not giving this to anyone but *you* from now on!"

He slipped two fingers between the hairy lips to tease her clit as he smiled and said, "At least we agree on some things. But can you afford to give it to a useless tramp like me?"

She sat up, using his semi-erection as a hand grip to help her, then gave it another playful jerk as she laughed and said, "I hardly call you useless, Deek. Your *face* is handsome, too."

He reached out for her, but she eluded him with another laugh and said, "Save it for later, after we have something to smoke and something to drink."

"Why can't you go out after we tear another, Kitten?"

"Don't be silly. My legs are wobbly, now. I wish to come one more time, and then I wish to smoke and sip and never move again. Who knows, we may even wind up *sleeping,* after we know one another better!"

He saw she was slipping into her simple peon outfit with amazing speed. So he laughed and said, "Okay, but if you're not back soon I'll start without you. What's the story, after? I can't stay here indefinitely."

She sat on the edge of the bed, in her blouse and skirt, tying her sandal, with one foot up on the bed between them as she asked, "Why not? Have you heard me ask you to leave? Do not concern yourself about having no money, Querido. I know ways to get money. I wish to share *everything* with you, no?"

Like other peon girls, Vivaracha wore nothing under her skirts. So with her one knee up like that he could see her groin if he moved his head a little to the right, and it was sort of weird that he wanted to, when you thought about it. He'd just had her, twice, stark naked, but the view up under her skirts seemed interesting in a teasing way. He ran his hand under the red folds and said, "Gotcha!" as he slid two fingers in. She squeaked like a goosed mouse and tried to cross her legs as she grabbed his wrist and protested, "Stop that! It feels so ... *wicked,* this way."

He sat up, still fingering her, and tried to lay her across the bed as he said, "Yeah, the grass is always greener. When you do it with your duds on you want to do it naked, and when you're naked ... "

"No," she said. "I don't wish to mess my clothing." Then, as she saw the condition of his shaft, she said, "Oh, I can see we must do something about that!"

Their hips were in opposite directions as he teased her with his fingers. So she simply dropped her head in his naked lap and took his shaft in one hand to lower her lips to it. She'd said she was dying for a smoke.

As she started puffing his piece pipe he debated returning the favor. She solved the problem by refusing, silently, to roll over in a sixty-nine position. He could tell by her contractions on his fingers that he was treating her the way she wanted. So he raised the hem of her skirt for a better view as he administered a skilled hand job while Vivaracha did a solo on the French horn. She must have found it novel to come fully clothed, too, because she beat him to climax, pulled away from his hand, and moved around on the bed until she was on her hands and knees between his legs while she sucked him like a lollipop. It looked lewd as hell with him naked and her fully dressed. He lay back, closed his eyes, and exploded joyfully in her pretty face. When he opened his eyes again she was on her feet again and saying, reproachfully, "Oh, you naughty boy. I can hardly stand up. If I wasn't already dressed I never would be able to go for our smokes and drinks. Is there anything else I can get you while I'm out?"

He doubted they sold guns at the hacienda, so he said, "Just hurry back with that sweet little body and, oh, is there any food in the house?"

"Of course. Have you forgotten I sell food at the marketplace? Tonight we shall dine on black beans and rice, unless you wish for me to make you some nice enchiladas."

"Honey, the only enchilada I'm interested in right now is the one between your thighs. Hurry back. I'm starting to get horny again already!"

She laughed and let herself out, leaving him alone with his confused thoughts. He'd read that some philosopher once said a man was only completely sane right after a warm meal and a good lay. He was sort of hungry, now that he had time to think about it. But he'd sure just had a good lay and, yeah, he did feel sort of sane and detached. So it was time to do some serious thinking.

He didn't know for sure if Gaston had gotten away or not. But since the little legion deserter was an older hand at this game than he was, it seemed more than likely. There was no way to contact Gaston without taking chances. So, okay, he could forget Gaston for now. If they both made it, they'd meet up again in Costa Rica, as planned. He was free to worry about making it there himself. Costa Rica was a couple of countries away and he didn't have a BB-gun or a plugged nickel, let alone the passport tedious officials tended to pester one about in these parts when they met a stranger.

He was safe for the moment, it would seem, with Vivaracha. But how long could that last? He wasn't given to false modesty. He knew he was a fairly good-looking guy and the gals down here liked the novelty of his blond hair and gray eyes. That had gotten him in lots of trouble since he'd arrived in this part of the world. The local hombres tended to act sort of nuts when the local mujeres started making goo-goo eyes at handsome gringos. He couldn't appear in public with Vivaracha without some local-yokel starting up with him, anymore than a colored guy back home could arm-and-arm it in a white neighborhood with a local belle. She'd said she'd give him some money. She sure was generous with her *other* gifts. But she wasn't likely talking about real money, since she was only a peon girl . . . . or was she?

He sat up, parted the netting, and looked around thoughtfully. He spied some vials on a dressing table across the room. He got up, walked over to sniff them and, yeah, he'd been right about her perfume being expensive. Rents were low down here, but you had to pay *something* for a place this size, and few pushcart peddlers made enough to even live alone.

He went back to the bed and sat down, muttering, "Okay, she sells more than peppers and papayas. But what?"

He'd already considered the wares she carried between her legs. If Vivaracha was a whore, he had to be better looking than he thought. No whores gave it away for nothing to a total stranger. She might have been out to wheedle him for money, afterward. But by now he'd convinced her he was really flat broke and she hadn't thrown him out. So that wasn't it.,

"Hey, maybe she just *likes* you." He shrugged. But that didn't explain how she got by so well in the world for a pushcart girl. He studied the spangles of sunlight on the floor, looking for a pattern. Not in the dots of light, but in the whole strange set-up.

He knew he'd pleased her in bed. But they'd never been to bed when she saved him from the British navy and . . . wait a minute! The schooner he'd been aboard had been run down by a British steamer. He'd been picked up by British navy men. And the last dame he'd met who acted so peculiar had been that agent working for Greystoke of British Intelligence, and The Bank of England was up to something here in Guatemala!

He shook his head. It wouldn't work. He knew the wiley spy-master master minding British Intelligence in Latin America liked to play involved chess games. But even if the Brits had known he and Gaston were aboard that schooner, they couldn't have anticipated him and the Frenchman surviving a deliberate hit-and-run. No, the arrogant skipper of the *Imperial Trader* hadn't been aiming at the schooner in that fog bank. He was just a nasty slob of the sea. The officers aboard the *Matador* might have suspected who he and Gaston were. He could put that on a back burner for now. That left Vivaracha. Had they *let* him escape under her cart for some devious Limey reason?

He shook his head. Not even Greystoke could have nubile female agents planted everywhere. They couldn't have foreseen when Gaston would make that break. So his meeting up with the mysteriously helpful Guatemalan girl had been pure chance.

She said she was a rebel. Could be. Could be a line to

see what *he* had to say about the local political situation, too.

He gasped, snapped his fingers, and got up to dive for his duds on the floor as he groaned, "Oh, you poor stupid asshole! *When* are you going to *learn*?"

He dressed in as great a hurry as he'd been getting out of the clothes. But as he put on the straw hat and headed for the door, it was already too late. As he reached for the latch, the door opened, and he found himself face-to-face with two gun muzzles. A brace of Guatemalan soldados were on the friendly ends of the carbines. Vivaracha was out on the pavement behind them, looking down and not meeting his eyes as one of the men covering him said, "You will come with us, Señor."

Captain Gringo nodded and said, "I guess I will, at that. You timed that pretty good, Vivaracha. It just occurred to me that you might be a police informer."

She murmured, "I am sorry, Deek, but a girl has to live. If you had had any money at all . . . "

"Yeah, I *said* I'd figured it out. Shall we go, caballeros? The sun is hot during La Siesta, and it seems to be making things stink around here."

It got worse. The streets of Puerto Barrios were deserted because of La Siesta. So there was no chance for a break as they frog-marched him to wherever, at gun point. The distinction between army and police tended to blur in Latin America, so he assumed they were taking him to the nearest police station until he saw they were approaching what looked like a small fortress. There was one gate in the long thick wall facing them. So if he meant to make a break, it was now or never. As he broke stride, one of them nudged him under the ribs with a carbine muzzle and he saw it was never.

They marched him inside and across a medium-sized parade to what had to be the headquarters building. Inside, he found Gaston seated in one of the arm chairs facing a fat officer behind a massive desk. The officer smiled up at him, indicated the remaining chair with a wave of his pudgy hand, and said, "So good of you to join us, Captain Gringo. As you see, Señor Verrier arrived ahead of you."

Captain Gringo sat down, but said, "I don't know what you're talking about. Who's this little guy, and who's this Captain whatchacallit?"

The officer dimpled and fondly replied, "Let us not play games eh? I am Major Llamas y Montana, Coastal Defenses. You, of course, are the notorious Captain

Gringo, alias Richard Walker, late of the United States Tenth Cavalry. We are sending you and your compadre, here, to our district of Naranjo."

Captain Gringo shrugged and said, "I'll bite. What's waiting for us at Naranjo, a chain gang or a regular jail?"

The major got to his feet with a sigh and said. "They told me you were a rather sullen type, even for a soldier of fortune. You really should learn better manners, Captain Gringo. It's no wonder you find yourself in so many fights. Please come with me, caballeros. I have something to show you as we discuss what you shall be doing in Naranjo."

As Captain Gringo and Gaston got up to follow him, the tall American noticed the carbine toting soldedos had left them alone with the soft looking major. Llamas had a revolver on his hip, but what the hell. The tall American asked Gaston what was going on and the Frenchman said, "I just got here, myself. It was a long walk back from the jungle."

The major opened a doorway to another room and they followed him into it. It was another office, with another desk, and a new-looking Maxim machinegun was squatting on it's tripod legs atop the green blotter. There were a dozen stamped steel ammo boxes in the far corner, but there was no belt in the Maxim's feed. So when Llamas asked him what he thought of the weapon, Captain Gringo stepped over to it, cracked open the breech, and said, "Head-spacing looks a little tight."

"Head-spacing, Captain Gringo?"

"Yeah, this adjustable block, here. That's the secret Hiram Maxim came up with after everyone else who tried to build a single barrel machinegun wound up with a blown breech. The newer Browning patent has it, too. As an automatic weapon heats up, the metal expands. So if you start out with a tight fit, something has to give. It's easier on the gunner's nerves if he gives the exploding ammo more room than if it tries to make its own by shoving the breech back in his face sort of sudden."

"Ah, I understand. We have to allow for something like that in our bigger guns. But that is why I was anxious to meet you, Captain Gringo. The machinegun, as you well know, is not a weapon many old soldiers are familiar with as yourself. You and Señor Verrier, here, are both said to be good field tacticians as well. Both skills will serve you well in Naranjo, eh?"

Captain Gringo frowned across the machinegun at him and asked, "Are you saying we weren't just arrested, after all?"

The major hesitated before he said, "Officially, of course you are under arrest, should anyone seeking to return you to Los Estados Unidos for trial happen to ask."

"I see. And, unofficially?"

"Unofficially, *very* unofficially, we want you to do us a small favor in Naranjo. We are aware of the considerable reward the U.S. Army has posted on you and of course the French government would like to have a serious discussion with Señor Verrier about the way he left his post under fire during that unfortunate Mexican adventure of Louis Napoleon a few years ago. We know that a short time ago you two were serving against us in the Honduras Army, too. But we Guatemalans are a forgiving breed, when people can be of *use* to us!"

He pulled a cord behind the desk and moved them back in his own office as he added, "I have sent for refreshments. Let us make ourselves comfortable as we discuss a delicate matter, no?"

They all sat down around his desk again and an orderly came in with coffee and iced biscuits. Captain Gringo had forgotten how hungry he was until he bit into one, wishing it were a steak.

Llamas poured his own cup last as he said, "As you may know, Guatemala is in a most unfortunate position with the Bank of England these days."

Captain Gringo washed his cake down and said, "Yeah, I heard you were in hock to them up to your eyebrows."

Llamas grimaced and said, "A very tedious race, the

56

English. They talk like mariposas and look down their noses at people they refer to as Tradesmen. To hear them, one would assume no highborn Englishman ever *thinks* of money. But when one makes a business deal with them, he finds himself in the greedy grips of a monster that would make an Armenian rug merchant blush for shame!"

"Yeah, they told the folks in India they were doing it for their own good, not the emerald and ruby mines. How do you guys figure to welsh on the Bank of England with a machinegun? I'm good. But not that good! If you're sending us to Naranjo to fight the British, forget it. Those Royal Marines don't talk like sissies and we've tangled with them before. The last time, we had U.S. Marines backing our play, and we still came out feeling nervous."

Llamas nodded, sympathetically, and said, "We heard about the Americans bluffing the expansion of the Empire to a halt in Venezuela. I assure you we have nothing quite so dramatic in mind. Guatemala is not about to go to war with the British Empire. We don't want to end up another British colony, and our credit rating is already low enough. That is the problem in Naranjo. The district is mostly uninhabited jungle, near the frontier we share with British Honduras. If we were to send our own troops in, *in force,* it could very well look like we were, indeed, biting the hand that feeds us."

Captain Gringo nodded and asked, "So what's going on in Naranjo and what are we supposed to do about it with one lousy machinegun, Major?"

The Guatemalan officer took a delicate sip of coffee before he said, "When we borrowed money from the British, they forced us to sign certain trade agreements. They said they were going to build a highway through the jungle from the seacoast of British Honduras at Belize, to open up our landlocked northern territories to international trade. The jungle products up around Naranjo are very rich, if one could get them to the sea. As it is, the territory is, as I said, almost deserted and very poor."

Captain Gringo nodded and said, "Yeah, and the Brits could likely find use for the chewing gum, rubber, and mahogany that would have to leave from the British port at Belize. Is that why you don't want the highway?"

"On the contrary, we want the highway very much. But you see, the British don't seem to be building it. They have gone back on many other promises as well, but none concern you and that machinegun in the next room as the situation around Naranjo does. You are right about them shipping mahogany from Belize. Victorian furniture seems to require lots of mahogany. More mahogany than there seems to be in British Honduras. So now they have started to steal *ours,* from the unguarded jungles around Naranjo."

Captain Gringo frowned and said, "That sounds pretty raw, even for Queen Vickie's gang. Have you complained to her about it?"

"Of course, and Whitehall was most *simpatico.* They said it was an outrage that anyone should steal valuable resources from a poor country trying to get back on it's feet after a series of economic disasters, but that, also, they could do nothing to help us. It would seem they do not feel responsible for mahogany pirates poaching our hardwood from across the border we share, alas, with British Honduras."

"Oh, come on, nobody's about to smuggle a whole damned tree past British Customs, and they have to be shipping them somewhere unless they just like to cut down big heavy trees just for the hell of it!"

The major nodded and said, "We know the timber they are cutting without paying Guatemalan forestry charges are leaving for English furniture makers via Belize. A ship called the *Imperial Trader* is docked there, now, waiting for another cargo. Naturally, we can't stop them from taking on cargo in a British port of call. The British Customs agents say there is no way to prove the logs coming out of the Honduran jungle were not cut there, as the mahogany pirates claim. One gathers the owners of the *Im-*

perial Trader went to the right public schools in England, eh?"

"Yeah, I know about the "Old Boy" network. Know about the *Imperial Trader,* too. This is one time nobody has to twist my arm, Major. We owe *those* sons-of-bitches! They're not just arrogant about little countries. They're arrogant about little *boats* too!"

Gaston said, "I agree les big shots have rough justice coming to them. But getting to a British merchant vessel docked in a British port sounds *très fatigue,* non?"

Major Llamas nodded and said, "I am giving you both direct orders not to move that machinegun across the border into Crown territory. They are most welcome to cut down all the mahogany in British Honduras, for all we care. Your job will be to stop them from cutting any more in *Guatemala!*"

Captain Gringo nodded and said, "Doesn't sound tough, if you give us a handful of guides and scouts who know the jungle up that way, Major."

Llamas looked like he wished Captain Gringo hadn't brought that angle up. "You shall, of course," he said, "have some other, ah, unofficial people with you. After that, it get's complicated. The mahogany pirates are not your usual rag-tag band of border jumpers. The cutters, of course, are English speaking Blacks from the British West Indies. They are led by a rather hard-cased band of adventurous whites, operating under the cover of pretending to be surveyors for the proposed highway. Most are English speakers like yourselves. We don't know if all of them are English. They may have recruited other soldiers of fortune, since the "Old Boys" don't like to do their own dirty work, and the jungles around Naranjo are dirty indeed. Aside from the usual insects and snakes, there is the Maya problem. You have heard, of course, of the Maya?"

Captain Gringo nodded and answered, "Slept with one a while back, further north. She was a great lay, but sort of primitive, now that I think back. I didn't know you had any Maya in Guatemala, Major. How many could be left, after your Spanish ancestors chopped them up in the good old Cortez days?"

Llamas looked hurt and said, "Don't be unkind, Señor. I see you share the usual misconceptions about the conquest. That is what comes of letting New England Protestants write your American history books. In the first place, Cortez conquered the Aztec, not the Maya, and if his methods seem cruel to you Anglo-Saxons, I'll thank you to remember that when Hernando Cortez arrived on the scene, the Aztecs were practicing cannibalism and human sacrifice on an astounding scale. My ancestors, it is true, may have burned a few Aztec priests at the stake, but that was after they found Spanish captives hanging from the walls of Mexico City with the hearts carved out of their living flesh with stone knives!"

"I read the Spanish version, Major. We were talking about Mayan Indians."

"Just so. The Maya were never molested by Cortez. Their days of greatness were long passed by the time Columbus discovered America. At one time the Maya ruled a vast lowland empire, or perhaps a confederacy, from the south of Mexico well down into Central America. They may have been more advanced than the later Toltec and Aztec civilizations, if one can call a culture indulging in mass human sacrifice civilized. One still stumbles over the ruins of their pyramids and temples in the jungle all around us. But, long before the first whites made contact with them, something happened to the Maya. It all crashed down like a house of cards, to be swallowed in Time and the rain forest."

"I remember now. What do you suppose it was, something like the Black Plague that hit *our* folks about the same time in Europe?"

Llamas shrugged and said, "*Quien sabe*? Once they had books. Our early priesthood, in its zeal, burned them all. No living Mayan can read the hieroglyphics on the stones still out there in the jungle. Naranjo seems to have been a religious center in the days of Mayan glory. The Mayan *people* did not die. Their culture collapsed, perhaps in a great unrecorded civil war that killed off their leaders. But we shall never know. The reason I can't assign any guides who know the country around Naranjo to you is that nobody lives around Naranjo but scattered bands of primitive Maya, and they are most . . . uncooperative."

Gaston said, "*Merde alors!* Does that mean, in addition to your mysterious mahogany pirates, we may have to fight *wild Indians,* too?"

Llamas didn't answer.

He didn't have to.

It took them more than a week to reach the Naranjo district with the machinegun, their pack mules, and the thirty-odd "people" Major Llamas assigned to them. The two squads of unofficial soldiers, well-armed but wearing peon clothing, had brought along their adelitas, or female camp followers. Captain Gringo and Gaston seemed to be the only guys in the outfit who were willing to sleep alone, and Gaston kept making dumb remarks about what a nice ass his younger comrade had. Gaston hadn't been able to get laid before the Guatemalan picked him up and drafted him.

The so-called road from Puerto Barrios to the vaguely defined Naranjo district was little more than a jungle path that didn't agree too well with their map. The further they went, the narrower it got, as the tropic vegetation crowded out onto it to steal some sunlight. Major Llamas had told the truth about it being rough country. Their point man was hit by a tree boa before they even got there. It was a bitch digging through the roots off the trail to bury him. The big snake had no poison fangs. The guy had died with a fractured skull when the tree boa's armored head punched into his skull like a big fist armed with brass knuckles. They didn't bury the boa. They ate it. Fresh meat was hard to come by in the jungle and after the adelitas cut it up and roasted it with peppers from the supply packs it wasn't half bad.

They lost one of the girls to something that looked like an asparagus from some giant's garden, armed with the thorns of a cactus. The girl just brushed against it with her bare shoulder on the trail one day. By the time they made camp that night she was feverish and her shoulder was a mass of pussy black, brown and green. Captain Gringo gave her some quinine and the others fussed over her most of the night. By morning she was dead. So they had to dig some more. Captain Gringo was anxious to *get* somewhere, for God's sake, so he took the lead, letting his peon followers work out the details of changing partners for the night. The dead lead man had left an adelita and the dead adelita had left a guy who didn't have one. So it seemed simple enough to him. But from the fussing he heard in back of him from time to time, the "widowed" adelita didn't like the left over peon all that much.

Late that afternoon, the trail ended. It didn't peter out. It just plain ended in a clearing around a big slab of limestone with lots of funny writing and spooky faces carved on it.

Captain Gringo took the map from his new but already trail-weary jacket and unfolded it as Gaston joined him. The Frenchman regarded the idol or whatever and said, "Ah, we seem to have arrived. Why do you suppose that stoneface is giving us dirty looks, my intrepid jungle explorer?"

"Probably someone he ate," Captain Gringo muttered. There's nothing like that on this map. If we're on this trail, here, it's supposed to keep going, not end up against any Mayan statuary."

"That sounds reasonable, Dick. Obviously, we're not on the trail we thought we were, hein?"

"Yeah, I think I see what happened. I thought I noticed a smaller foot path running off at an angle a couple of days back. How was I to know that was the main trail, and this was the side road? This one looks more well-travelled."

Gaston stepped over to the Mayan carvings and ran a thoughtful finger over the stone before he said, "There would be lichen and more shit of the birds on this thing, if it had been standing like this, abandoned, for five or six hundred years. I think the reason the trail looks well-travelled is because it *is* well-travelled. I thought by this time most of the Maya would have been converted to Christianity, or least burned at the stake, non?"

Captain Gringo put the map away and took out a pocket compass as he said, "They told us some of them like the "Old Time Religion." This must be some sort of sacred spot, and we'd better get out of their church before they notice us!"

He held up the compass, squinted along the needle, and added, "It's not so bad. Wrong trail or not, we're still aimed more or less at where the damned fool map says Naranjo ought to be."

Gaston stared soberly at the wall of trees the taller man was sighting and protested, "Surely you jest, my old and rare! We have lost two people out on the open trail, and now you suggest we plunge headlong into such wicked salad?"

"Come on, you and I have been through some rain forests before. You know the underbrush is always worse along the trails. We were only following that trail because we thought it *led* somewhere! The going will be easier and cooler under the canopy."

He turned to the others, bunched up and watching from the edge of the clearing. He called out, "Follow me!" and put the compass away, heading for the tree line. They did so, reluctantly, and some of them made the sign of the cross or pointed forked fingers at the sinister pillar of limestone in the clearing as they passed it.

As Captain Gringo had foreseen, once he was through the wicked thorny growth along the sunny side of the tree line, the jungle, or rain forest, opened up into a cathedral-like gloom. The massive trees on buttressed roots shaded the soggy soil too much for serious bushes. You could see much farther despite the greenish gloom, and it was easy to walk between the big trees spaced four or five yards apart. The ground under his boots felt like wet black paper pulp and smelled like rotting garbage. From time to time he had another glance at his compass and he seemed to be leading them in a straight line north, but he kept checking anyway. They couldn't see the sun, save occasional shafts of light lancing down high above through breaks in the canopy of green. There was no slope to the ground to indicate direction, either. One tree looked pretty much like any other, so it would be easy as hell to get turned around and lost in here. When he cautioned Gaston about this, the Frenchman snorted and asked, "*Merde,* what do you mean we *could* get lost? We *are* lost, you species of imbecile! Has it yet occurred to you how easy it would be to swing east? None of the others with us would know."

Captain Gringo frowned and asked, "Why the hell would we want to go east? British Honduras is over that way."

"Ah, you noticed, hein? British Honduras and the sea both lay invitingly to the east. I share your distaste for the master of that steamer that ran us down and drowned everyone with us on that poor little schooner. But you are going the wrong way, Dick. We shall find the *Imperial Trader* in Belize. Why don't we get out of this fatiguing jungle and just sink the damned tub so we can be on our way, hein?"

The tall American shot another compass heading, saw they were drifting to his right, and said, "Two reasons. One we made a deal, right?"

"*Mais non,* we were pressed into service at gunpoint, so all bets are, how you say, off? It's true the major issued us revolvers as well as the machinegun. It's true he even provided us with fresh clothing and a little expense money.

But did you hear him say anything about really paying us for all this work?"

"He said we get a thousand apiece and Guatemalan passports, if and when."

"*If and when* indeed! He did not trust us to come back if he gave us any real presents. So why disappoint him? Let us hire ourselves to more civilized climes and let them do their own fighting, non?"

"No. I wasn't finished. There's a second reason. That Vivaracha I told you about was probably just a police informer. But we did escape from the Royal Marines, so by now British Intelligence must be wondering why Guatemala hasn't got around to shooting us or claiming the rewards on us. That means our old chum, Greystoke, knows we're in the area. We'll see if we can do the job we signed on for. Then we'll see whether Llamas doublecrosses us or not. We know Greystoke's done so, often enough."

He pushed on north, ignoring Gaston's bitching, and a few minutes later he spotted something white on the ground ahead and moved in, slow, wondering what the hell a white woman was doing naked on her back in the jungle, for Pete's sake!

Then, as they got closer he saw it wasn't a human body. It was a white stone statue of a lady with enormous breasts, flat on it's back and smiling serenely up at the forest canopy. There were Mayan hieroglyphics covering her otherwise nude body, like lace. Some of the writing was mutilated as if it had been hammered by a rock in an angry fist. A long time ago, from the patina on the stone. A big glob of water splashed down on the face of the Mayan goddess or whatever. As he looked up, he could see why the stone was still white after all this time. The overthrown statue lay in a dripway that probably came down like a firehose during the rainy season. He looked around at the black forest duff before he said, "They don't pray to *this* one anymore. Remember what Llamas said about a long-forgotten civil war?"

"Mais oui, she must have been a deity of the losing side. Too bad. I admire her figure and she has a much pleasanter expression than the one back there someone still seems to respect!"

As they were talking, some of the others edged closer. One of the mule packers said, "Forgive me Captain Gringo. I am sure you know where you are going and the major said for us to follow you. But this is *Brujo* country, and my people are afraid!"

The American commander of the little expedition said, "The Maya are not witches, ah, Pablo. They're just pagan Indians. This looks like some kind of fertility goddess. You can see it's been abandoned a long time."

Pablo forked his fingers at the fallen idol to ward off possible evil eyes as he replied, "Perhaps, my captain, but one can see they still make sacrifices to the *other* one we saw! Maya are most savage. Not even the ones who say they are Cristianos can be trusted!"

Another man made the sign of the cross and said, "*Es verdad*! In my village there was once a Mayan woman, married to a Ladino. The goats did not give milk. The chickens did not lay eggs. Some pigs and even a child got sick before we drove the Bruja Maya away with stones and curses!"

Captain Gringo grimaced and said, "I'm starting to see why they live in the jungle. We're not here to fight the Maya, damn it."

"I agree, Señor. But what if they wish to fight us?"

It was a good question. Captain Gringo didn't have a good answer, so he said, "All right, we've all seen the pretty dolly. Let's pick it up and move it out! It'll be getting dark, soon, and I mean to find a decent place to make camp."

As he started to turn away, one of the adelitas pressed forward and asked if she could have a private word with him. Captain Gringo said she could if she could talk and walk at the same time. So she fell in at his side but didn't say anything as she waited for them to put some distance between themselves and the others. She was the adelita of the guy who'd been killed by the snake. She was short and plump, albeit nicely curved. Her berry brown face was almost pretty, and though she'd probably never owned a bottle of perfume, she managed to look neat and clean in her thin, faded cotton blouse and circle skirt. Her bare feet were broad from growing up barefoot. But she carried her plump little form gracefully, her muscular calves tapering to very well-turned ankles. She said her name was Picantita and that she had a problem. He thought her titas were very nice indeed, so he asked her what it was.

Picantita said, "You know my poor José was killed by that terrible tree boa. And Pablo lost his adelita to blood poisoning, eh? It is the custom for every man to have an adelita, and for every adelita to have a man no?"

He nodded and said, "That's the way it usually works. What do you and Pablo want, my blessings?"

"Oh, *no, por favor*! Pablo is ugly, and his breath smells bad!"

Captain Gringo hadn't thought the mule packer looked all that great, either, but Pablo's looks were hardly anything he could do a thing about.

Picantita sniffed and said, "The others say if I do not give myself to Pablo, you will make me leave the guerrilla. *Es verdad*? I have nowhere to go in this frightening jungle, Captain Gringo!"

He rolled his eyes heavenward and muttered, "Why *me*, Lord?" before he told her, "Don't worry, Picantita. Nobody's going to abandon you in any jungle. I brought you along, whether it was my idea or not, so I'll get you back to Puerto Barrios, knock wood."

"Does that mean I do not have to be Pablo's adelita?"

"Not if you don't want to be."

"I don't. If I am not to be Pablo's adelita, who's adelita am I to be?"

He grimaced and said. "Don't look at me! I have enough to worry about! You just adelita anybody you want. But drop back to the main column and don't pester me about it."

"Can I tell them I am your adelita, for to keep Pablo's hands out from under my skirts?"

"God, no! I told you you could still tag along. But I want you to go on cooking and making yourself useful to my guerrilla, not starting fights. You'd better not flirt with any of the others, if Pablo can't have you. In the first place, the others have adelitas and I don't enjoy watching women fight, either, and in the second place, any man you chose over Pablo would be an insult to his manhood and while he may not be pretty, he's big and sort of mean looking!"

"Oh, he *is* mean, Captain Gringo! He used to beat his other adelita before she died. That is why I would not wish to be his adelita, even if he did not have such a vile breath!"

"You've told me all that. Move it on back and stay out of trouble, or I will leave you sitting on a log with a can of beans and two matches."

She blanched and ducked away from him. Gaston, who'd been listening in, moved closer to observe, as they strode on side-by-side. "Well, as I see it, my adorable youth, you have two choices. Are you going to shoot her or are you going to shoot Pablo? Since it must be one or the other. I suggest you shoot Pablo. The girl has a nicer ass, and Pablo will be annoyed at you either way!"

Captain Gringo sighed and said, "Let's not hope it's that serious."

"*Merde alors,* how many times do you have to find yourself in such a situation before you learn, my incurable optimist?"

He slipped on some wet forest duff, cursed, and added as they walked on, "When I was young I sometimes wished nature had favored me by making me one of you tall blond-savage types. Since meeting you, I see I was *très* fortunate to be my own adorable self. I never would have lived this long the other way. Does it not get tedious,

69

having women fight over your body, my poor unfortunate youth?"

"Knock it off, Gaston. I'm not after that chubby little mestiza and you know it."

"*Oui,* but does *she* know it, and, more important, does *Pablo* know it? He is big and mean, but not as big and mean as you Dick. So when he makes his move, you shall not receive the usual warning bluster."

"Tell me something I don't know, damn it! I understand the situation. God knows I've gotten *into* it often enough down here! I just don't know what to *do* about it! Your suggestions sound pretty ruthless, even for you."

Gaston laughed and said, "*Oui,* but who would use ruthless methods if they did not work so well, hein? You have the rank to make it stick if you killed him first, for insubordination or something."

"I know. Call me a soft-hearted slob, but I've never been able to kill a man who hadn't done anything to me yet."

"The yet is the topic under discussion, Dick. Once that little adelita tells them she prefers you, and she will, he'll either have to go for you or slink away with his tail between his legs. You may have noticed this is not good country for slinking."

"I know. I still have to let him make the first move. He must know *you* wouldn't just stand there like a big-ass bird if he hit me from behind."

"I doubt he thinks that far ahead, Dick. Even if I kill him, after he kills you, what good will that do either of us? I'll miss you, sweet companion of my declining years! I'll tell you what, if you don't want to kill Pablo and claim the girl, let me do it. I don't have bad breath and she looks fine to me!"

"Negative to both suggestions. I sure wish there were some hills around here. How do you suppose the natives get around in a country with no landmarks?"

Gaston shrugged and said, "They obviously do, or they would not leave trails for innocent travellers to get lost on.

But you have made a good point in my favor, Dick. How are we to know when we reach Naranjo, and even if we know we're in the area, how are we to find our mahogany pirates? The jungle is, as you say, nearly featureless. They could be poaching timber only a few miles away without our being able to tell, and the area to be swept is huge, as well as wooded."

Captain Gringo spotted a modest patch of bare red soil ahead and answered, "I'll explain later—after we make camp. I thought we were moving up an almost imperceptible rise. It's late and the ground here is as dry as it's likely to get in this fucking forest."

He moved into the biggest, albeit modest, opening between the massive hardwood columns and raised his hand for attention as he called out, "All right, everybody circle up and listen sharp. We're making camp for the night here. Pablo, front and center."

The burly mulepacker came forward, leading his mule and looking confused. Captain Gringo hadn't made any sub-leaders up to now. It was a good idea to know your men, down here, before you passed out any rank. The thing that made guerrilla life so interesting was that everybody wanted to be a chief and nobody wanted to be an Indian. So as soon as some guys moved up a notch on the pecking order, they tended to puff up and get arrogant and difficult. Captain Gringo nodded at Pablo and said, "You're older and more experienced than most of the muchachos, Pablo. So I'm putting you in charge of setting up camp. You know how I want it done, right?"

Pablo grinned, exposing an alarming gap in his teeth as he replied, "Sí, My Captain! Several small fires instead of one big one, with the night guards on picket outside the glow of the campfires, right?"

"Right. I thought you looked like an old soldado. What sort of outfit were you in before Major Llamas assigned you to this punitive expedition?"

Pablo looked puzzled and answered. "Outfit, My Captain? I was in no outfit. I was a bandito, before they caught me and said if I did not wish to be shot I would have to be a soldado with you."

"I see. Carry on, Pablo. Gaston, you and I will scout the perimeter while the sergeant, here, sets up camp."

As the two soldiers of fortune walked away, they heard Pablo crowing, "Hey, you chicos and chicas hear that? I, Pablo, am a sergeant! Morillo, take charge of this thrice-accursed mule! I am too busy a man to lead any mule, eh?"

As they got out of earshot, Gaston muttered, "Nice try, Dick, but I don't think it will work. In the first place he's a moron, and in the second, I fear it's a little late to make friends with him!"

Captain Gringo snorted and said, "I thought you said you were an old soldier. I'm not trying to make friends. I'm giving Pablo a chance to make some enemies!"

Gaston brightened and said, "Ah, I see the method in your madness. If and when he starts up with you, it will be a fight between leaders, just between the two of you! Very sneaky. But you were going to tell me how on earth you intended to stumble over a modest logging operation amid all this adorable vegetation, non?"

Captain Gringo stopped by a huge tree that looked like a California redwood that had somehow wandered into a tropical rain forest and sprouted live oak leaves. He patted the massive trunk and said, "This is mahogany."

Gaston stared up at the column losing it's top somewhere in the overhead green canopy and said, "I take your word for it, my botanical comrade. But as you Yankees say, so what?"

"So look at that big bastard and tell me how you'd pick it up and carry it, once you chopped it down!"

"Ah, oui, one becomes *très fatigue* just thinking about cutting through a bole that thick, and mahogany is heavy wood in any dimensions."

"You got it. Llamas didn't say anything about a road, let alone a railroad. So the only way anyone could move enough mahogany to matter would be by floating it out.

There are three rivers large enough to be on the map in the Naranjo area. They all drain east, across the border into British Honduras. As flat as it is around here, the so-called rivers are probably more like long skinny swamps. But we'll find the mahogany pirates logging near one or the other. Probably the biggest and deepest, since the choice is theirs. The map doesn't show much detail, so we'll have to cut across all three, figure out which is the best for floating mahogany logs, and move downstream until we stumble over them."

"Why downstream and not upstream, Dick? Is there some law of nature that says timber poachers can't cut anywhere they wish, as long as they have water to float the timber on?"

"Yeah, the law of gravity. They haven't been cutting on this side of the border long and we're moving in line with the border, well inland. These mahogany trees grow widely spaced, but how far west could they have worked in two years, right?"

Gaston frowned and said, "Two years? I don't remember Major Llamas saying how long this business has been going on. I thought it had began more recently."

"Maybe Llamas thought it had. That police snitch, Vivaracha, told me her home village had been wrecked by loggers a couple of years back."

"*Oui,* but she lied to you when she said she loved you, too."

Captain Gringo started to object. Then he frowned and said, "When you're right you're right. She must have been padding her part when she played malcontent to see if she could pump me about what we were doing here in Guatemala. Major Llamas said nobody lived around Naranjo but some left-over primitives, and Vivaracha was white, or almost white. So she or the major was fibbing, and Llamas had no reason to bullshit us."

They moved on, making a wide circle around the campsite as they gave the others time to set it up and scouted all the approaches. There wasn't any particular direction from which to launch an attack. Captain Gringo had chosen well. The campsite sat on modestly high and dry ground. Anybody who wanted to do something about that could of course move in from tree to tree after dark. But the trees were widely spaced with no ground cover between them and if the night guards didn't go to sleep they seemed as safe here as anywhere else.

As they headed back to join the others, they saw the orange flicker of a small cooking fire between the trees ahead. "Good," Captain Gringo said. "You can't spot firelight from any great distance in this neck of the woods."

Gaston shrugged and said, "*Oui,* but what about the howler monkeys?"

Captain Gringo frowned, cocked an ear, and said. "What are you talking about? I haven't heard any howlers, Gaston."

"Neither have I, since just before we came to that stone pillar, earlier today. Does not this make you wonder, Dick?"

It did, now that he thought about it. The ubiquitous noisy howlers of the Central American lowland jungles had started cussing from the trees at them from the moment they'd entered the jungle days before until, as Gaston said, this very afternoon. The howlers were harmless, for all that noise they made, so after a while one tuned them out. But the howlers never seemed to get used to human company and as one passed under each troop's home territory, they took up the bitching with fresh enthusiasm until one's human ears learned to ignore them. Captain Gringo looked up. The canopy above was getting even darker and though they couldn't see the sun, it had to be setting. "Maybe they knocked off early for the night," he said. "Howlers don't yell in the dark. It gives those big monkey eating owls too nice a shot at them."

Gaston insisted, "It was too early when we stumbled over that Mayan shrine. I think we hear no howlers in

74

these parts because there *are* no howlers in these parts, Dick."

"Meaning someone's been hunting them, right?"

"Exactly. One has to be an Indian to fully enjoy a meal of ugly monkey. Remember how those Jivaro to the south shot them out of the trees with their poison darts?"

"Yeah, but I don't think Maya use blowguns. I read somewhere about them going in for long skinny spears they threw with a sort of paddle."

"*Oui*. So tell me, collector of occasionally useful information, would you rather be hit by a blown dart or a spear propelled by a throwing stick?"

"Ouch, either way! You're probably right that someone's been hunting the noisy bastards enough to make them shy about announcing their whereabouts. But nobody hunts at night, we've got repeating weapons, and the Indians may be friendly. So what the hell."

By now they'd reached the campsite. Captain Gringo nodded approval at the way the fires and sleeping bags were spread in a big circle with the mules tethered and nosebagged in the center. Pablo or someone had placed the Maxim machinegun near one of the fires, so Captain Gringo joined the four men and their adelitas seated on the ground around it. One of the women had put coffee and a pot of something that smelled good on the coals. As the two soldiers of fortune hunkered down, Gaston asked, "Do you think we should set the machinegun up, Dick? I see no belt in the feed."

Captain Gringo shook his head and said, "No. I don't want the canvas ammo-belts to get wet if it rains tonight. That Maxim would be useless in any case, if we got hit among all these trees. Why waste ammo in a hand-to-hand situation?"

"Oh, you have just cheered me up immensely! Heads up, your old friend Pablo is headed this way with a machete!"

Captain Gringo got back to his feet and casually opened his jacket, in case he needed a fist full of revolver in a hurry, as the burly ex-bandit came closer. Pablo had the machete down at his side, but that didn't mean much, if you knew how the guys down here could handle a machete.

76

Pablo tried a half-ass salute with his free hand and said, "As you see, my Captain, we have gathered plenty of firewood and I took the liberty of choosing the first night pickets. They did not wish to stand out there away from the fires and their adelitas. But I reminded them I was your sergeant and only had to hit one of them."

Captain Gringo nodded and said, "Good. I'm leaving the details of such matters to you, Sergeant."

Pablo smiled, but asked, "May I have a private word with you, My Captain? It's a personal matter."

Captain Gringo nodded at Pablo, shook his head at Gaston, and led the bearish peon off into the trees to get it over with.

As soon as they were alone, Pablo sighed, "I have a problem with that stuck up adelita, Picantita, My Captain. She says she does not wish to be my adelita. I feel gravely insulted. Do I have your permission to simply rape the silly puta into submission?"

Captain Gringo shook his head and said, "That could set a bad example. You know how nervous some men get when there's a rapist around their own women, Pablo."

"I was afraid you'd say that. But what am I to do? I do not wish the others to laugh at my manhood, and I was foolish enough to make a public statement that she was to be adelita."

Captain Gringo nodded sympathetically and said, "Hmm, you do have a serious problem. You may as well know that Picantita has already spoken to me about it, Pablo. She asked me to tell you to leave her alone. I said it was none of my business. I am not a man who fights over women."

Pablo looked relieved and asked, "*Es verdad*? You have no idea how good it makes me feel to hear this, my Captain. The stupid bitch has been telling the other women she wishes to be your adelita."

Captain Gringo laughed, keeping his gun hand on guard anyway, as he said, "I thought she looked like a troublemaker. You seem to be a man of the world, Pablo.

I'll bet this isn't the first time a prick-teaser has tried to get you into a fight, right?"

"Alas, My Captain, that is all too true. I confess I never have been known for my looks, but a man has his honor to think of. I know it's that puta's doing, but even so, if the two of you made me look like a cabron, I would have no choice but to fight you!"

Captain Gringo was an easy going cuss and so he was willing to bend, to a point. But not if it meant letting a not too bright peon get the Indian sign on him. So he said, softly, "Watch it, Sergeant! When I said I wasn't one to fight over a woman, I didn't mean I was *afraid* to! So listen sharp, you stupid pobrecito! I haven't tried to take your girl away. I don't want the little bitch. But if you're trying to be a hero, he advised I've handled bigger hombres than you in my day. So simmer down and let's talk like grown men instead of schoolboys about the situation!"

Pablo blanched and said, "*Por favor,* I do not wish to fight with a man of your reputation, Captain Gringo! What I meant was that some of the others are expecting me to. You know how my people are about such matters."

The tall American sighed and said, "Don't I ever! You have to stroll into the paseo in a strange town wearing blond hair and an Anglo face to really savvy the Hispanic taste for melodrama. I notice your people like to watch bulls bleed. So what do you suggest we do about Picantita? I can't let you beat her into submission and it seems sort of mean to desert her in the jungle."

Pablo nodded and said, "I can see that, my Captain. What if I were to sell her to you?"

"Say again?"

"Sell my rights to her," Pablo insisted, explaining, "She is mine by right of custom. So I would be honorbound to fight any man who took her from me, even if she does say she is not my adelita. But since she is mine,

I have the right to sell her. That would put the sandal on the other foot, no? For then *I* would be the one who was rejecting *her!*"

"I can see how that might work," Captain Gringo laughed. "But as long as she's your property, can't you just give her away?"

"Oh, no, My Captain. Nobody ever *gives* a woman away. People would think he had no head for business, and that is almost as bad as being a cabron!"

Captain Gringo nodded, sagely, as if he understood. "Cabron," literally, meant a billygoat. Up to now, he'd thought it translated into English best as "pimp" since the idea was a man who willingly wore horns. A guy whose wife cheated on him behind his back was only a fool. A cabron was a guy who *allowed* it, hence the insult. But maybe selling a woman like livestock didn't make a guy a pimp in Pablo's cultural niche. It was probably something left over from the days when chattel slavery had been legal down here instead of just customary. He asked, cautiously, "Ah, how much are you asking for the girl, Pablo?"

"I had not considered it up to now. Are you making me an offer, My Captain?"

"Maybe, if the price isn't too steep. I don't want the dumpy little bitch. But if you think selling her to me will restore your honor, I'm willing to do you a favor—as an amigo."

Pablo looked like a man reprieved from a death sentence, which he was when you thought about it. He said, "Price is unimportant, between *compadres-in-arms*. You don't have to give me any real money, if I have your permission to tell the others I sold her to you for a hundred quetzales."

That came to about ten bucks in U.S. money, so Captain Gringo said it sounded reasonable and held out his hand to shake on it. Pablo shifted the machete to his left fist to take the taller American's right in his. Then, as they smiled understandingly at one another, the burly mestizo tried to take Captain Gringo's head off with a left-hand machete blow!

It had been a pretty slick notion but, unfortunately for Pablo, he was dealing with a pro who'd run into it before. As Pablo had supposed, he couldn't go for his shoulder holster with an idiot holding his right hand, but he still had his left free. So he dropped under the swing and pulled Pablo forward off balance as he shot a left hook into Pablo's rib cage, knocking the wind out of his body and the machete out of his suddenly paralyzed fingers. As they both fell to the soggy jungle floor, Captain Gringo got his right fist back. But as he was first on his feet again he didn't use it. He proceeded to kick the shit out of the man on the ground with his big mosquito boots!

Pablo blubbered, covering his face with his hands as he pleaded, "*Por favor*! I was only joking! I do not wish to fight you!"

Captain Gringo kicked him again and asked, "Who said you knew how, you asshole! You had your chance to settle it the easy way. How do you like mine, you son-of-a-bitch!"

Pablo tried to grovel out of range, toward the machete a few feet away but Captain Gringo drew his gun, took careful aim, and shot Pablo in the nape of his thick neck, blowing bloody froth and shattered teeth out the other side.

By the time the body had stopped twitching and he'd reloaded the .38, Gaston and some of the other men had run out from camp, attracted by the gunshot. Holding the gun down at his side, Captain Gringo pointed at the corpse at his feet and said, "It's over. You were right. He wasn't very bright."

One of the peons rolled Pablo over and whistled softly as another made the sign of the cross. Captain Gringo asked, "Does anybody have any personal questions?"

There was a general shaking of heads and the man who'd rolled the dead man over said, "No, My Captain.

He told us he was going to get you. One can see his mouth was a better fighter than he was."

"Gee, thanks for warning me, muchachos. It warms my heart to see I'm among friends!"

The man who'd crossed himself looked reproachfully and murmured, "It was not our place to get into a personal matter between officers."

"I understand. One question, and I want an honest answer: are any of the others likely to feel they owe anything to Pablo's memory?"

"Oh, no, Señor. You have not tried to take any of *our* adelitas away."

Captain Gringo started to say he hadn't even wanted Pablo's, but he let it drop. They might take it as weakness if he looked like he was sorry about what happened. Guerrilla leaders weren't supposed to feel sorry about killing anyone they felt like killing. He nodded and told them to fetch some shovels from the supplies. As they left him alone with Gaston, he said, "See you don't mess with any of their women, Pard. Do you want that fucking fat girl? I think I just won her in an affair of honor."

Gaston sighed, "I would like fat fucking very much indeed, but she's told the other women she's in love with you and they'd expect you and I to fight next. She's all yours, Dick. You'll have to pay for killing Pablo with the mortification of your flesh."

Captain Gringo grimaced and said, "I wouldn't touch her with your prick, now! Jesus H. Christ, we've lost two men and a girl and we haven't even reached Naranjo yet!"

Captain Gringo awoke from a wet dream wondering where he was, how he'd gotten there and who the hell he seemed to be screwing, for, as his head cleared, he saw he hadn't just been dreaming that part!

He'd gotten into his sleeping bag naked, of course, and the girl he seemed to be on top of didn't have a stitch on either. The campfire a few yards away had smoldered to ruby coals, so even at close range, he couldn't make out the features of his unexpected bed partner. But he was half-way to climax and she was moving her firm plump body skillfully. As she clamped down on his shaft and moaned, "Oh, I am coming, Querido!" he knew who it was. He'd said he didn't want to lay Picantita, but this was a hell of a time to argue about it!

He exploded in her tight moist flesh before he muttered, still atop and in her, "Well, hello there. Who invited you to come to bed with me?"

She giggled, "I came in bed with you indeed! *Madre de Dios,* you are hung like El Toro, Querido mio! I was frightened when I saw how big it was, but once it was in me you made me very happy."

He started to withdraw, but then he noticed how good it felt right where it was and, what the hell, the fat was in the fire, so he started moving, slowly, but said, "I ought to take you over my knee and spank you, Picantita. Your nonsense cost me another man. There's no way to send for any replacements, either."

She raised her knees to grip his rib-cage with her heavy brown thighs and take him deeper as she said, "Pooh Pablo was fat and stupid and you saw he did not know how to fight. But I am so happy you fought for me. It is a great honor to be the adelita of a commanding officer!"

"Oh? Is that why you threw yourself at me, Picantita?"

She started to move her firmly fleshed rump as she replied, "I think I love you most because you are tall and handsome, but I am glad you are also in command."

He started to tell her to watch that "love" bullshit, but if he were in command of the punitive expedition, it was up for grabs just who was in command in this sleeping bag. Picantita's firmness of flesh and slender waistline kept her from being what you could really call fat, but she was certainly pleasantly plump, and they didn't need a pillow under her fanny to present her hungry little love maw at a very interesting angle for serious rutting. His knees could feel the hard ground under the sleeping bag —everything else he was laying on was soft and springy as a feather bed. Her breasts against his bare chest felt like firm eggplants, with perky teasing nipples added. He didn't think it would be a good idea to throw the covers off and get acrobatic, with others sleeping all around.

But even though he was still annoyed at her or, well a *little* annoyed, Picantita was one of those rare women who didn't have to change positions much to keep a man interested. He kissed her to keep her from babbling dumb things about love, and she kissed great, too. He knew he'd hate himself in the morning, but it was incredible how well their totally diverse bodies fit together. She seemed to move instinctively, just right, and his leaner body fit comfortably in her warm brown curves. She didn't seem to have a bone in her body. She was all filet mignon as well as a fille de joie, and it was about time something started going right around here.

She started moving wilder as she tongued him with his

lips on her soft rosebud mouth. She was one of those natural, primitive girls who came easily and often. She was no troublemaker at all, in bed. He joined her in mutual orgasm as she moaned and raked his back with her nails while she drummed on his buttocks with her heels and tried to suck his tongue out by the roots. When they came up for air, she sighed and said, "Oh, that was divine. But get off me for a moment, *por favor*."

He knew he was a big guy and assumed he was a bit heavier for her than the men she was used to. He kissed her again and rolled out of the saddle onto his back, grinning, as he reached out a naked arm to grope for a smoke from the clothes he'd left beside the roll when he'd climbed in, expecting to sleep alone.

But before he could get to his shirt, Picantita h.. ..rown back the covers and forked a thick little thigh across him to do it some more with her on top. He started to protest they might be seen by someone, but as she settled on his half-erect shaft and drew it to full attention with her pulsating tight vagina, he decided there wasn't anything to be ashamed of. Let anyone who noticed eat their hearts out. She was a fantastic lay in any position!

Pretty, too, now that he had a better view up at her in the cherry red glow of the distant embers. She got her bare heels under her center of balance on either side of his hips, and, bracing her elbows on her knees, started playing squat tag on his stalk with her short strong legs folded and spread at an astounding angle. It felt as wild as it looked, and it looked wild as hell as she bounced up and down like a dancing Cossack, smiling down at him, eyes closed sensuously. He noticed her big firm breasts didn't flop as she moved up and down. He folded his hands on the back of his own neck to luxuriate in the way she was sort of jerking him off with her whole body at once. Having an adelita of his own was going to weaken his position if he wasn't careful. Like a priest, a military leader seemed more potent if he betrayed no human appetites. But if he had to have a goddamn adelita, it wasn't as if he'd wound up with an ugly one, one that didn't know how to please her man! She threw her head back and began to swing it from side to side, brushing her own naked back and thighs beyond with her long black hair as she moaned. "Oh, you were fashioned by the angels to fit in me just right, Querido! Do you like what I am doing?"

He said, "I love it. But aren't you getting tired up there? You'd better let me get on top again before you cramp your thighs."

She straightened up, laughing, and smiled down at him as she said, "Too late. I just came that way. But you can finish on top if you wish. I shall always do anything you wish for me to do, Querido! Now that I have found you, I wish to be your adelita forever."

Picantita didn't get her wish. Before he could even answer, she stiffened and clamped down hard on his shaft, and it took him maybe a full second to realize what had happened as he stared up in horror at her.

A long slim spear was sticking out of both sides of Picantita's head after going clean through her skull!

As she started to fall forward on him, staring blankly from wide, dead eyes, Captain Gringo shoved her pretty naked corpse the other way, pulling his erection out of her dead, but still sensuous-feeling vagina, and was out of the bedroll and yelling, "Indians!" as he rolled over to his clothes and got his gun!

His shouted warning drew another spear, but since he'd kept rolling as he snatched his .38, it missed and stood vibrating on its point in the earth. He had no muzzle flashes to fire back at. But he slid like a reptile on his naked belly into the shadows afforded by the winglike buttress roots of a nearby tree. So even though another spear thunked into the bole above him, he was now as invisible as the unseen enemy. He sat up, braced his back against the tree and the .38 across his drawn up naked knees, and tried to figure out what was going on.

He could see the dead adelita between his position and

the campfire coals. That was all. He thanked his lucky stars they hadn't hit earlier, when the fires had been brighter. Somewhere in the night, guns started going off, so he knew the others were awake and aware. After that it was up for grabs. He cursed himself for being a fool. He'd expected any attackers to be armed with guns that flashed in the dark. Nobody had informed him the fucking Maya thought they were Apache, for God's sake! The bastards were supposed to be shy slash and burn farmers who *avoided* Cristianos! What the hell could have riled them up?

Somewhere in the night, a woman screamed. But he couldn't see what was going on. Apparently the attackers couldn't either. He flinched as a stocky dark figure, outlined v the firelight moved cautiously into view, not looking is way. The Maya had no idea where he'd holed up. The v moving in for a kill had a spear cocked in the throwing stick above his right shoulder. In his free hand, he carried a paddle-shaped hardwood club, studded with stone teeth to finish off anyone he might hit with that damned spear.

Captain Gringo raised the muzzle of his .38. Then he hesitated. The guy wasn't coming at him, and there were others, probably on the far side of this very tree. He knew he was giving his position away, but you don't win fights by hiding like a rabbit in it's hole. So he held his breath, steadied the revolver against his knee, and fired.

The Indian jerked like a puppet on a string and fell on his face with the spear doing a head stand between him and Picantita's sprawled nude body. Captain Gringo just had time to note he'd nailed the son-of-a-bitch through the spine when another guy whipped around the buttress root, waving another of those wicked clubs and apparently yelling rude things about Captain Gringo's mother!

The gun was quicker than the club. The second Indian staggered back with a .38 round in his chest, dropped the weapon and flopped on his back.

The third one he saw didn't seem to be after Captain

Gringo. The Maya dashed into view, ran to the nearest body, and grabbed it by the ankles to haul it back into the jungle. It seemed a shame to shoot a medic, but Captain Gringo was pissed off about Picantita. So he shot the bending Indian in the ass and, when he straightened up with a howl, shot him again more sensibly.

For a while nothing happened. Captain Gringo hadn't brought spare ammo along, so he couldn't use the lull to reload his .38. Which was a shame, in a way, since he only had two bullets left. Like most savvy gun-toters, he let the firing pin of his double-action revolver ride on an empty chamber. It saved accidents, but right now he sure would have liked to have that sixth round.

Nothing happened for a while longer. He knew from his Apache fighting days back home that when Indians started trying to pick up their casualties, they were thinking about pulling out. Of course he meant sane Indians. The ones who'd just busted up his sex life had no reason to attack, which meant they were unusually truculent, which made him nervous. He'd lost a trooper, back with the old Tenth Cav, to an Apache who didn't know the attack had been called off. So he stayed put, sweating out another rush with two lousy rounds in his gun.

He heard Gaston calling his name, somewhere in the dark. He yelled, "Stay put! If *I* can't see you, they can't see you! How did you make out, Gaston?"

"Not too well. Two of the people around me took spears. But I think we have driven them off, for now. What's the plan, Dick?"

It was a good question. Up to now, he'd just been planning to stay alive a few more minutes. He figured spears would be thudding into his tree right now if anyone on the other side was close enough to matter. So he ran from the tree, leaped the smoldering campfire, and joined Gaston and some of the others on the far side, knowing he was now invisible from the jungle side. Nobody commented on his nudity. A couple of the men and one woman had been rousted out of bed naked, too. It didn't seem important at the moment. He saw they were near the mules, in the center of the fire ring, and hence no target for the nasty but short ranged spears. He called out, "Everybody on our side, rally on my voice, *muy pronto!*"

As others moved cautiously toward Captain Gringo, some gasping in pain from spear wounds, Gaston stood up and said, "I've had some of the fires put out with drinking water, thrown from this side."

Captain Gringo nodded as he made a quick head count. Then he swore. He couldn't tell the hes from the shes in this darkness, but he'd started out with over thirty people and he had sixteen heads, besides his and Gaston's! He said, "All right, muchachos y muchachas. I don't need to tell you we're in a fix. I nailed three of the bastards. Anybody else get one?"

A couple of the men said they'd nailed a Maya, or thought they might have in the lousy light. He said, "So they've taken some casualties. They've withdrawn to make more medicine and talk it over. But we've the best part of the night ahead of us. If they're serious about this business, they'll give it another try before it's light enough for our superior weaponry to count."

"Agreed," Gaston said, "but with the fires out, and us all on the alert, they will have a hard time over-running us, non?"

One of the men, who apparently really had been in the army one time, spoke up to suggest, "What if we form a circle with the mules and supplies, shoot the mules to use them for shields, and dig in behind them?"

Captain Gringo said, "We'll have a mess of dead mules. I brought them because I didn't want to carry the supplies on our backs. Aside from that, they'll have us nicely bunched in a small circle. They're not shooting bullets at us, so your barricade's a good suggestion for soldados or banditos. *But not for Indians.* I need some volunteers. You, you, and you two, I want any bodies you can find and all the weapons out there, including my machinegun and ammo boxes, hauled in here by the mules. Oh, yeah. I want my sleeping bag and clothes, too. Bring Picantita and her duds along, too. What are you wating for, a kiss goodbye?"

As the "volunteers" dropped to all fours and started crawling off in all directions, Gaston observed, "I can see why you would want your pants. I agree we should salvage the weapons. But why are we to worry about our dead at a time like this, Dick? Even if the Indians mutilate them, what can it matter to them, now?"

Captain Gringo said, "I'm not just being sentimental. There's method to my madness. I told you I expect those bastards to make at least one more try under cover of darkness and I even have a good idea which direction they'll come from. They hit us from the east, last time. So the next time, they'll attack from the opposite direction, from about due west."

"How droll. No wonder your Apache are back on the reservation! I, too, know the strategic sense of savage generals. But, even if we foresee the direction of their next attack, they have us at a considerable disadvantage, here, non?"

"If you'd just shut up and listen, I'd tell you my own strategy, damn it!"

So Gaston listened and when Captain Gringo had explained his plan, the little Frenchman laughed, "How Machiavellian as well as droll! You realize of course, that if it doesn't work, we are all dead,"

"I do. Have you a better plan?

"*Mais non,* just so you realize I think yours is *très risque!*"

It took over an hour and considerable oration from the war chief to get the Indian raiding party to even consider another attack. Then a scout came in, standing politely silent until the chief bade him speak, and said, "It is as you thought, Ocelot Who Dances. The trespassers on our sacred land think they have driven us from the field like frightened puppies. They have moved closer together in the center of their camp, of course. But unless they are foolish, even for Cristianos, they don't expect us to hit them again. They are sitting around a big fire, like they make. They must hope the firelight will keep us at bay, as if we were the animals they say we are. I did not see any other pickets, like the ones we picked off the last time. But I moved carefully, as you told me to. It is possible they have scouts of their own out. But you know how poor their night vision is and . . . "

Ocelot Who Dances held up his hand for silence, saying, "I told you to scout the enemy. I did not ask for advice on how to kill them."

He turned to the other dimly visible forms around him in the darkness and added, "I, Ocelot Who Dances, mean to pay them back for our fallen brothers. This time it should be easier, since we have them all bunched up and plainly visible. Is there anyone here who is afraid to go with me?"

Nobody answered. Some were afraid, but Ocelot Who Dances was said to walk in the footsteps of the war gods of the Grandfather Times. So he had to know what he was doing.

The war chief grunted in satisfaction and started moving through the trees, spear in one hand and Mayan sword-club in the other. Like most of his followers, he was dressed in the simple cotton shirt and stagged breeches of the more typical peon. Since the Grandfather Times, his people had adopted habits of the strangers that made sense. But instead of a straw sombrero, Ocelot Who Dances wore a head dress of green tall feathers from the sacred quetzal bird. For this was more serious business than the corn in the milpas around their unmapped village to the north. Ocelot Who Dances meant to keep his village off the map of the Cristianos. Being on a map meant paying taxes, and enduring the men in black robes who insulted the gods of the Grandfather Times.

The Maya hadn't run far, so they didn't have far to go before Ocelot Who Dances saw the glow between the trees. As he had instructed his followers, they'd reformed cleverly on the west side of the camp. Ocelot Who Dances walked in the footsteps of the war gods and knew all about tricking the enemy.

He moved closer, keeping an eye peeled for Cristiano pickets. But his scout had been right. There were none. The foolish strangers thought Mayan warriors gave up easily. He could see them, now. As the scout had said, they were hunkered around a great fire, like children afraid of the darkness. Some were lying down; others were probably talking about the fight they'd had a while ago. The chief searched the bare ground inside the firelight's range. He didn't see the man he'd lost and he felt bad about that. If the Cristianos had buried them, without proper Mayan rites, he would look for them in the morning light, after they killed all the Cristianos.

He stopped between two trees in the darkness just outside the camp. Summoning his men closer, he said, "I shall take the lead. Be careful not to spear me by accident. You are all good men. You can see what has to be done. They are in a tight circle around that fire. So even a boy could hit at least one of them, launching with his eyes closed! We shall throw our spears in one volley as we charge, then finish them off with our sword-clubs. In the name of Invincible Jaguar, let us hit them *now!*"

As the others followed, Ocelot Who Dances charged forward, spear cocked, chose his target and launched it with his throwing stick. The spear flew hard and straight, with a flat trajectory, and the war chief grunted in satisfaction as he saw a man fall forward without a sound.

Other spears whizzed past him on either side, lancing into the hated strangers with audible thunks, like a machete biting into flesh. And then Ocelot Who Dances was on top of the enemy before even one of them had reacted, his sword-club slashing down at a man still seated, crushing his skull, as other Maya followed suit. Ocelot Who Dances leaped the fire, raising his weapon to smash another enemy, who just sat there, face blank, not moving. The Mayan war chief frowned and muttered, "What's this?" and nudged the man with his sword-club. Nothing happened. The fool just sat there. He was *dead. All* of them were dead!

"It's some kind of trick!" shouted Ocelot Who Dances. And then, before he could shout an order to retreat, Captain Gringo opened up with the Maxim from the darkness to the north!

Ocelot Who Dances was one of the first to die, since the Yank with the machinegun recognized a chief when he saw one, even by firelight. Hot Maxim rounds blew Ocelot Who Dances off his feet and into the roaring campfire, where his pretty feathers went up in a puff as his bleeding flesh sizzled on the flaming coals. The others with him didn't make out much better as Captain Gringo hosed the machinegun back and forth like a scythe of streaming lead. It wasn't the scientific way to use a machinegun, according to the instruction books, but it sure chopped the hell out of the attacking Maya!

The few he missed went down as Gaston and the others opened up with less dramatic but well aimed fire. A wise ass Maya ducked behind a seated adelita and tried to use her as a shield. It didn't work. The men who'd propped her up there with crossed stakes under her dress knew all too well they couldn't hurt her further by firing a fusillade of hot lead into her corpse and the live Indian behind her. So that left him dead, too!

"Cease fire!" Captain Gringo called out, his ears ringing from the roar of his own now silent weapon. He left the Maxim where it was to cool as he drew his revolver and moved out into the light to double-check. He counted thirty-odd dead Indians. So they'd killed two for every one of their own casualties and probably wiped out the band, since that was about the average number of any war party he'd ever tangled with.

He rolled a body over with his boot. The Indian looked too young to die and was dressed like a simple peon farm boy. But his features were pure Indian and nobody was ever *old* enough to die, so what the hell.

Gaston joined him to say, "Eh bien, it worked better than we had a right to expect. What next? Do we move back in and bury the dead? Some of them are beginning to look a bit shopworn."

Captain Gringo shook his head and said, "No. Keep everyone but a work detail back in the dark with the mules and supplies. We'll prop up the dead, throw some more logs on the fire, and see if it will work again."

"*Merde alors*! Do you really expect yet a third attack, Dick?"

"Not really. But Napoleon wasn't expecting that sunken road at Waterloo, either. If there *is* another war band anywhere in the neighborhood, they can't get at us if we lay doggo in the dark with our guns cocked. We can stay awake until morning and let them catch up on the cooking and sleeping in broad daylight, where the odds are even."

Gaston nodded, but said, "I am pleased to see you have learned to be more cautious, Dick. But we are not going to make much time moving half a day, and one can see the futility of travelling through this jungle in the dark."

"Okay, so we'll walk faster in the afternoon. We haven't even made it to the first river, yet."

"*Oui,* and already we have lost half our strength. I told you his was going to be *très fatigue.* At the rate we're going, we shall have no choice but to drop this nonsense and run for the coast, before it is too late!"

Captain Gringo and his handful of survivors were not molested further by Indians as they shivered through the night with guns trained on their mock camp. They weren't shivering because they were frightened, even though some of them were scared skinny. They were cold as hell.

It sounds crazy, but pneumonia is a leading cause of death in the tropics. It never gets really cold, of course. But when it drops to less than sixty degrees on a damp night, and you're wearing soggy cotton far from the campfire, it feels like someone should be ringing jingle bells.

By morning, some of the undernourished peons were coughing and hacking up phlegm and Captain Gringo noticed goose bumps under his linen jacket. The decoy fire had subsided to embers by the time it was light enough to see they had this patch of jungle all to themselves. He put his people to work digging graves, partly out of respect for the dead and mostly to warm them up. He stayed by the dew-covered machinegun while they buried Picantita and the others. He had a grim enough picture of the way she'd looked with that spear through her head. He didn't want to remember such a great little lay as a bullet-torn mess.

He'd told Gaston they'd rest during the day, but this was ridiculous. After they'd tidied up the massacre scene he headed them out through the cathedral-like gloom. Gaston kept saying they were lost. Gaston was most likely right. But he had to get everyone warmed up and dried out, lost or not. He knew that if he let his tired people lay down clad in thin cotton and goose flesh some of them might not ever get up.

As he trudged by the side of the pathetic column, he saw that the attack had been rougher on the men than their adelitas. The reason was easy. The men had been the ones who jumped to their feet when all those spears came whizzing in from the dark. He had six men and nine women left. None of the pack mules had been lost or injured, so they had plenty of supplies to share. But, Jesus, how were he and Gaston to take on an illicit logging operation with half dozen followers?

Gaston was wondering that, too. When he asked, in English, the tall American said, "We salvaged all the guns and ammo. We'll have to enlist the girls as fighters, too."

"*Merde alors,* it's not the custom for adelitas to fight, Dick. They only came along to fuck."

"So we'll change the customs. They joined up for adventure, right?"

"Perhaps, but I wish I shared your faith in such small a species of Amazon. It's true we did meet the real thing down in South America a while back, but these peon girls seem *très* delicate for jungle warfare!"

Captain Gringo shrugged and said, "Don't be so old fashioned. People don't fight with broadsword and battle axe these days. A dame can pull a trigger just as easily as anyone else. When you get down to basics, a modern soldier is just a gun with a human attached to it to move it around. So if we can whip these adelitas into shape we'll wind up with two corporal's squads of infantry."

Gaston grimaced and added, "How disgusting to think of warfare as just another middleclass trade. I hope your droll ideas don't get around. I foresee some nasty wars in the coming century if they simply start drafting the great unwashed and sending them to the front for on-the-job training, hein?"

Then he brightened and continued, "but perhaps we shall stay lost and never have to prove your outrageous theory. Now that we have more than enough women to go around, I can think of a better use for at least a couple of them. I shall train my own recruits in the skills of Eros while you try to reach the arts of Mars. I say *try,* of course, because it is impossible to turn a peon girl into an infantryman, Allah be praised!"

The light was getting better. Either the sun was getting higher or the canopy above them was thinning out. Captain Gringo yelled out that they could slow down a bit, since he'd noticed his own goose bumps were gone as his muscles warmed up. He told Gaston, "We've got to find some open high ground and get a line on where the hell we are. The asshole who drew our map must have been guessing a lot. They sent me into Apacheria with a lousy map one time, too. Someone in G.H.Q. must have liked me. They gave me a lousy map and a platoon of troopers they must have wanted to get rid of, too. I told you the old Tenth Cav was a colored unit with white officers. Some of the older non-coms were ex-slaves. The others were on share-cropper farms for the most part. Most of them couldn't read or write, and when I got them most of their training had consisted of cleaning out stables for white troopers. So there I was, chasing Geronimo with a faulty map and a mess of untrained colored kids."

Gaston shrugged and said, "You must have seduced some colonel's wife. Is there a point to all this, Dick?"

"Yeah. I'm still alive, and Geronimo is sulking on the reservation some more. The other white officers felt the same way about my privates, then, as you feel about our adelitas. Who'd ever heard of a colored soldier? They were supposed to be good for nothing but picking cotton. When I took over my platoon most of my men were hell bent on proving the wise money right. They were sullen, bewildered, and the Apache made them almost as nervous as snakes, and you should have heard what they said about *snakes*!"

"You told them there were no snakes in Apache country?"

"I told them there weren't any hoop snakes or death mambas in Arizona, and that the Apache were more dangerous than a few old sidewinders. I had to bullshit a lot and bang heads together a little and by the time we *did* tangle with Apache, guess who won?"

Gaston looked over at the rag-tag column staggering with the mules, mostly wearing skirts, and said, "I have watched you whip outfits into shape, Dick, but this is *très ridicule*! If I were you, I would be headed due east, for civilization. The women should be a welcome addition to British Honduras, since they are seeking colonists. You, myself, and the men left ought to be able to avoid arrest until we can work out some more sensible moves, hein?"

Capain Gringo shook his head and said, "You're not me. This jungle doesn't stop short at the border, you know. The towns and plantations along the seacoast are farther away right now than Naranjo."

"*Oui,* but nobody is waiting there to shoot us, since they do not know we are coming.

"The mahogany pirates up around Naranjo don't know we're coming, either."

Gaston shook his head and said, "I wish I shared your optimism, Dick. That Major Llamas would seem to have been planning this mad expedition long before he recruited us, if what the others tell me about being scraped together from various farms and jails is true. Gossip is a major form of entertainment down here, and if I were running an illicit logging operation in Guatemala, I would certainly have *my* ear open to Guatemalan gossip!"

Captain Gringo didn't answer. Gaston was probably right and he was bitching enough already. He saw a bigger than usual shaft of sunlight lancing down between the trees ahead and said, "The canopy's thinning out. Come on, we'd better scout ahead."

The two soldiers of fortune picked up their pace and left the others behind as they moved in step with the pack mules. Less than a mile to the north, a wall of brush rose like a hedge before them. Captain Gringo noted, "We've come to a river or a clearing. Damn, I should have brought along a machete."

But he hadn't, so they had to bull through the hard way and when they had, they saw they'd come to both. A broad but shallow stream of tea brown water rolled sluggishly before them. On the far side, the land rose higher and was semi-open savanna. Waist high grass covered the open ground between clumps of brush and trees. Way off to the north, a little solitary tree covered butte loomed against the sky.

Gaston nodded at the waterway and said, "*Eh bien*. We have reached river numero uno. If we can ford it without being swallowed alive by some *très* unpleasant creature, we can scout along the higher bank to the east, non?"

Captain Gringo shook his head as he took out his map. He said, "Look at the current. It's running the wrong way, to the west, inland! There's no way anyone could float timber down it to British Honduras."

He unfolded the map, studied it intensely, and added, "This river isn't supposed to be here at all."

Gaston broke off a twig, cast it in the water to make sure the current wasn't an illusion, and said, "Perhaps rivers don't read maps. Or perhaps since it obviously runs into some inland lake or swamp even deeper in the jungle, the mapmakers did not feel it was important, hein?"

"I don't think the sons-of-bitches ever surveyed this area properly. That's the trouble with these little banana republics. They claim as much land as they think they can get away with, and don't have the populations to settle a tenth of it. I think we can trust the border lines on this dumb map. We're in a panhandle big enough for Texas, with British Honduras over to the east and some unsurveyed territory claimed by Mexico to the north. Everything else is up for grabs. The real village of Naranjo might be within a hundred miles of this dot on the map. But if it is, where the hell is the so-called road we're supposed to be on?"

He put the map away, shot the sun with his watch and compass, and said, "Run back and hurry the others along. The sunlight across the river will dry us all out and we'll make for that hill over there to see if we can get our bearings."

As he waited, Captain Gringo experimented with fording the river. The water only came to his knees. He hadn't taken off his boots. He was fond of his toes. So when he got to the sunny side, he paced up and down to squish the water out of his mosquito boots and, after making sure he seemed to be alone, he took out the little book he'd picked up in Puerto Barrios before leaving.

When Major Llamas had mentioned Maya in the area, Captain Gringo had thought it might be a good idea to know something about Maya. Knowing a little about Apache had saved his life a couple of times. The book was obselete by about five hundred years, but so were any Maya still living wild in this primitive area. The Spaniard who'd written the book had no idea, either, why the Mayan civilization had fallen apart about the time of Charlemagne. But for a time traveller's information, they'd been pretty weird Indians. They'd built pyramids to rival Egypt's, but they'd never invented the wheel. Their priesthood had worked out a calendar better than anyone was using right now, and could predict eclipses hundreds of years ahead. But they'd sacrificed virgins to a bewildering pantheon of nightmare gods who made devil worshp seem almost reasonable. They shared the Great Feathered Serpent with the Toltec and Aztec, though they called him "Kukulcan" instead of "Quetzalcoatl." By either name, he was a blood-thirsty son-of-a-bitch, even for a god. Captain Gringo couldn't figure out why they called him the feathered serpent, since he was supposed to be a human who'd somehow changed into a god. The ancient Greeks and his own ancestors had turned humans into gods and saints, of course, but not into mile-long snakes covered with feathers. The early Spaniards had been confused on this point, too. When Cortez marched into Mexico, a lot of the fight had been knocked out of the Aztec when their priests told them the armored Spanish adventurer was the great feathered serpent, back from his mythical home in the sea. Cortez must have looked pretty scary, dressed in shiny steel and packing a gun as well. But a snake with feathers . . . ?"

He put the booklet away as Gaston and the others started fording the stream to join him. He told them they were making for that distant butte. One of them looked around, nervously, and said, "This land has been cleared, My Captain."

"I noticed. Nobody seems to be farming it at the moment, though. It could even be a difference in the soil. See that flat outcrop over there? The bedrock's only inches below the surface, so the trees only grow in scattered pockets of deeper soil. But however the jungle was thinned out, let's find out where the hell we are!"

He took the lead, heading for the only high ground he could distinguish. As the others struggled after him, Gaston fell in step at his side and said, "We should have flank scouts out, Dick. I don't like this savanna country. Those tree-covered hammocks on all sides offer endless opportunity for ambushes, non?"

Captain Gringo nodded, but said, "We'll worry about training new scouts when we find out where we are and set up camp in a strong place. Those Indians separated the men from the boys when they knocked off the guys I'd detailed to guard us last night. The ones we have left are the slackers who stayed down when the egg hit the fan. I hope some of the adelitas will shape up better. Meanwhile, we know those spears don't travel far and it's easy enough to stay out of range of the brush clumps."

"I'm not worried about being speared in broad day-light. A rifle bullet can kill at over a mile. But I see you have forgotten the mahogany pirates, hein?"

"I haven't forgotten them. You've forgotten why they're called *mahogany pirates*. There's no mahogany growing out here on this savanna. Those big trees are thirsty buggers and this is dry, shallow laterite soil. Besides, I told you we'd find them cutting near some stream, running the right way."

The steep butte they were making for was farther off than it looked, and once they'd dried out under the tropic sun, the sun started to overdo a good thing by trying to bake them like potatoes. But they kept picking them up and laying them down and at last they got to the butte.

But it wasn't a butte, now that they were up close. Captain Gringo stared up at the high steep-sided pyramid and whistled softly as he thought of all the sweat and toil that must have gone into piling all those big blocks of limestone in place. The rains of a thousand years had blurred the carvings covering the stone and the patient roots of the brush and gumbo limbo trees growing out of the cracks had split and shifted the blocks as well, but it was still an imposing monument to the monster gods of the Mayan civilization.

A steep stairway of pistachio green stone ran alarmingly to the summit. So Captain Gringo told the others to hold the mules and started its ascent, with Gaston naturally tagging along, apparently in order to bitch.

"*Merde alors!*" he panted, half-way up. "It's no wonder their civilization fell apart. They must have all died of heart attacks, if this was their idea of a staircase!"

Captain Gringo didn't answer. Gaston had a point. Some of the green stone risers had been dislodged by roots and one uncalculated step could send them both down the steep stairs, all the way. The pyramid's sides set at more than a forty-five degree angle, made it higher than it was broad at the base, and it was pretty impressive at the base.

He hauled himself onto a flat space at the top as a lizard skittered away to duck into what looked like a little tollbooth squatting on the truncated top. It seemed one hell of a climb to get to such a little church, if that was what it was. They couldn't read the hieroglyphs over the door, but the writhing two-headed dragon with a human skull in each of its mouths probably meant the building had been important—once.

He hadn't come up here to study archeology, so he ignored the cubical mini-temple to gaze out across the country he could see from up here. The river they'd forded meandered off to the western horizon. The horizon was blurred by the high humidity but as far as he could see, it seemed flat. There were isolated distant bumps that could have been hills or other ruins, if only he could make them out. Far to the west-north-west he saw what was either a mirage or a vast sheet of water. He took out the map, consulted it, and said, "If that's Lake Peten, and they have it right on this dumb map, we're south-west of Naranjo and south-east of Tikal."

"Let's go to Tikal, then. I would rather meet up with a cantina than mahogany pirates, any day!"

Captain Gringo put the map away as he said, "You haven't been able to buy a drink in Tikal for a thousand years. It's a Mayan ghost town. Llamas says the Maya living around the ruins of Naranjo are semi-civilized Christians, when asked. They trade a little with the border town of Yaloch.

"Let's go to Yaloch, then. Maya make me *très* nervous."

"I noticed. Yaloch's beyond Naranjo and the people there are Indians, too, with a small garrison of Guatemalan border guards. The mahogany's not being smuggled across there. Not because you can't bribe border guards, but because it's high and dry around Yaloch. I'm beginning to wonder about Naranjo, too. Have a gander over there to the east, Gaston. Is it my imagination, or would you say the horizon is a little *higher* toward the border?"

Gaston squinted into the distant haze, shrugged, and said, "I can't tell. I need my reading glasses, perhaps. The one river we've found most definitely runs the wrong way, non?"

"Yeah, so what the fuck are we doing here? If the drainage in these parts runs deeper into Guatemala, how could anyone be rafting logs down to British Honduras?"

"Perhaps there is a pass allowing at least one river to run the other way. On the other hand, perhaps we have been sent on the chase of a wild goose, hein?"

"That makes no sense, Gaston. Why would Major Llamas want to do that?"

"Perhaps he does not like us? We have been crossed double before, you know."

"Boy, do I ever! But that won't work, Gaston. They had us under arrest and helpless, back in Puerto Barrios. You don't issue guys a new machinegun and turn them loose if you want to just get rid of them."

Gaston said, "You figure it out. I am going to have a peek inside that droll little building to see if they left any wine. After a thousand years, it should be nicely aged, hein?"

As the Frenchman headed for the corbeled doorway of the squat stone cube, Captain Gringo said, "Don't horse around, damn it! We haven't time to play in haunted houses!"

But Gaston called back, "It seems to be only one small chamber with pornographique illustrations," as he ducked inside. Captain Gringo swore and walked around to the far side to see if he'd missed anything.

He had. He took out the compass to make sure and, yes, that string straight line of oddly shorter grass was running back toward Naranjo. It looked like a long forgotten and shallowly buried highway had been built from this forgotten ruin to the ones around the better known ones at Naranjo. He nodded in satisfaction. The modern mapmakers in Puerto Barrios might not know the country up here, but the ancient Maya must have. If they followed the buried road, it would lead them via the best route to Naranjo. He remembered how that lost Inca road over the Andes had led through the lowest passes, and by drinking water and sheltered campsites.

Gaston called from the nearby doorway, "Dick? You'd better come in here. I want to show you something."

The tall American stepped over to the doorway, snorting, "What now, damn it? We haven't time to explore ancient ruins, Gaston. I think I just spotted a beeline for Naranjo."

Gaston said, "I think *I* have spotted something, too!" as he struck another match in the gloom of the windowless little temple. By the flickering light, Captain Gringo saw baroque nightmare figures writhing all around on the walls. Dragons, jaguars, eagles, and monsters too crazy looking to name were tearing the shit out of smaller human figures. The carving was shallow bas relief, but the vivid colors added three dimensional depth to the scene. As the flame scorched Gaston's fingers, he shook it out and said, "How long would you say paint should last in this climate, Dick?"

Captain Gringo nodded in the gloom and said, "Not a thousand years. Not such bright colors. So, okay, some of the local Indians come in here once in a while to touch up the carvings with fresh paint. So what? We know they were in the area, and they proved last night they're not Christians."

Gaston said, "It gets more interesting," as he struck another light and held it over an obscene stone figure in the center of the chamber. The statue was half life-sized and looked like something between a big frog and a little naked man, reclining on its back with a stone bowl in its lap. Gaston pointed down at the bowl which was filled with what looked like black bean soup, covered with flies. Gaston said, "They didn't feed this particular god a thousand years ago, Dick. I'd say the last time was no more than a few days ago!"

Captain Gringo nodded and said, "I'd say you're right.

It seems at least one Indian still honors his old gods with an occasional pot of bean soup."

Gaston lit another match as he shook out the one he'd been holding and gingerly stuck it in the bowl. The flies buzzed around his hand as he stirred the almost back skum with the match, and then held it up to the light, asking, "Do you call this bean soup, Dick?"

Captain Gringo didn't. Not once he'd seen the crimson goop Gaston had dug out from under the crust of fly-covered scab. As an old soldier, he knew there was nothing it could be but blood. Human blood. The blood of farm animals or game was other shades of red. The bowl in the lap of the ugly little god was big enough to hold a couple of gallons—and it had been filled almost to the brim by someone, recently.

Good military planners are flexible and the change in terrain called for rethinking, so Captain Gringo decided to take advantage of the ruins. The overgrown pyramid site was spooky. But whatever was using the little temple couldn't get at them by broad daylight without being seen on the open grass all around. Meanwhile they had cover and firewood. The canteens, of course, had been refilled back at the river. So Captain Gringo posted a lookout topside and told the others to make camp in the shade and spend the siesta sleeping instead of fucking, because there would be a full moon tonight and he intended an all-night march on the open savannah.

As he unrolled his own sleeping bag near the machine-gun he'd set up near the base of the pyramid, a delegation of two left-over adelitas came over to discuss that part with him.

They were called Juanita and Ynez. Juanita had a face that wouldn't have been pretty even if she'd had good teeth, but her body was fantastic. Ynez had a pretty little face with aristocratic cameo features left over from some early Spanish drifter who should have been ashamed of himself, if she'd inherited her build from the native girl he'd messed with. She was skinny, runty, flat-chested, sway-backed, pickle-assed, and bow-legged. Together, the two of them would have added up to one damned nice-looking adelita, but Juanita needed Ynez's face, or Ynez needed Juanita's body, depending on who you were looking at.

Juanita, the bolder of the two, said, "My Captain, the other girls wish to know what is to be done about so many of the men being killed."

He straightened up, leaving the bedding half unrolled, as he replied, "We buried them, and I already told everyone I was sorry as hell. After we've all had some sleep, but before we leave here, I'm going to show you girls a few things about loading and firing guns."

Juanita said, "We already know how to handle guns, My Captain. Most of us grew up around guns. For our mothers were adelitas, too."

"Good, it saves time if the trade runs in the family. I want you girls to turn in and get some sleep, now. We've got a long night on our feet ahead of us."

"Sí, you told us before. Marching is no problem for any adelita. We were born to march. But we were born for other things, and that is the problem. There are now about two adelitas for every hombre in the band. The two of us in particular have no hombres left at all."

He noticed Ynez had hunkered down to finish unrolling and smoothing his bed roll. That seemed reasonable. But then she slid out of her thin cotton shift to slide under the covers, which didn't. Jesus, she had a funny ass! Her little bunlike buttocks stuck out like tits stuck to the base of her boney spine. He saw Juanita was raising her arms to undo the ribbons of her long black hair, which made *her* stick out too! He said, "Wait a minute, muchachas. I don't want you to think I'm a sissy, or not greatly honored, but it's broad daylight and I want everyone to get some sleep!"

Juanita seemed to be doing all the talking, although Ynez seemed the one in the hurry as she smiled shyly up at him from under the covers. Her face was so pretty it was tempting, but unfortunately, he'd seen her naked, awful body. Then he started seeing more of Juanita's body than he'd expected to as, having dropped her hair down around her waist, she, too, began to peel her clothes away like she was shucking corn as she said, soothingly, "It is still early. We shall sleep better after we decide about the bigger problem, no?"

He sighed and said, "I can see you two have already decided," as he started to unbutton. He knew he really shouldn't be doing this, but now that Juanita had her clothes off he doubted there was a normal man on earth who would have turned her down. Her face would still stop a clock, but who looked at faces when there was almost five feet of breathtakingly beautiful tawny nude attached to it, below the chin?

Since they'd come as a team, he didn't ask foolish questions about who wanted to be his adelita. He undressed and got in the bedroll between them, asking, "What if someone comes?"

"We both intend to!" Juanita said, and then they were both all over him, rubbing against either flank as one or the other took his confused shaft in hand to straighten things out. He laughed and muttered, "Oh, decisions, decisions!" as he got an arm around each of them to snuggle everyone in one big cuddle under the covers. The sheet, thin flannel blanket, and canvas top were designed mostly to keep the night mists off, so it wouldn't have been so warm in here if he'd been alone in the shade of the gumbo limbo clump he'd chosen to stretch out in. He didn't want to be seen acting so familiar with the troops, and he was afraid he wouldn't be able to do right by Ynez if he had to look at her flat chest in broad daylight. So, what the hell, sweat added lubrication, right?

He started exploring with his hands under the covers as the two girls took turns kissing him while one or the other played with his dong. Juanita's breasts felt as good as they looked. Ynez didn't have what you could really call breasts. It felt like someone had pasted stuffed olives on a skinny teen-aged boy. But kissing a face that pretty was great. So, since he was fully aroused, he twisted out and up from between them, moved them closer together, and tried an experiment.

It worked good. He rolled atop Juanita's lovely heat-slicked body while kissing pretty Ynez. Juanita reached down to guide him into even nicer terrain between her shapely thighs as Ynez tongued him passionately. He hissed in pleasure as he sank into Juanita's lust box while, trying to be a fair-minded gent, he ran his free hand down the other girl's skinny frame to at least give her a break with his fingers. She felt pretty down there, too. She'd grown up with an androgynous build because they hadn't fed her right as a baby; not because she was undersexed! He was pumping wildly in Juanita as the statuesque adelita bounced her tail on the firm earth under them, and Juanita had a vagina that went with a great body. But Ynez was smaller in every way. Two fingers were enough to smooth out all the slack in her smooth moist opening, and from the way she moved her own hips, and moaned as she kissed him, she was enjoying herself as much as the one he was actually laying.

He had to get some of that. But that would mean mounting an ugly body and kissing an ugly face, if he wanted to be even-handed with them!

He'd have to study on that. Meanwhile, the sheer novelty of this earthy, uninvolved situation was just what the doctor ordered for a growing boy. So he grew even harder and let himself go as he saw they were both coming, too.

Ynez beat everyone to orgasm, which was sort of odd, considering. Her funny pickle-ass presented her vagina at an interesting angle and he imagined she wasn't as used to getting anything in there as often as the statuesque Juanita. Back home in the States, it was hard to tell what a gal had to offer under all the duds Queen Victoria said they had to wear, which was probably why Queen Victoria dressed so warmly, and a pretty face had trapped many a man into bedding a lady with piano legs. Down here, the guys had a better view of what they were getting into, so under normal circumstances, flat chested gals with pickle asses tended to be left out. But these were not ordinary circumstances. Since Juanita was starting to come now, he took his lips from Ynez, closed his eyes, and kissed Juanita as he gave her his undivided all. They came together and either that or the fact his eyes were closed made kissing her quite nice. He ran his other hand down Juanita's tawny curves, withdrew, and started petting her still throbbing groin as he shifted over on to Ynez next door. For the first time, she spoke aloud in a mousy little voice, gasping, "Oh, *por favor,* it is too big!" as he settled into the saddle between her open skinny thighs. She was right. If he hadn't still been all the way up he'd have gotten it past her little love gates. As it was, he almost needed a shoe horn. But then he was in to the roots, and as Ynez started bouncing on her funny little butt, he saw that whoever had said meat was more tender close to the bone must have made it one time with someone like Ynez.

He went on kissing Juanita, running his hand over her lush curves from breasts to groin to keep from remembering what her face looked like. Her pursed lips were lush and moist. Even ugly girls could kiss good, if they got the chance. The next time he had his hand in the hot wet thatch between Juanita's shapely thighs, she grabbed his wrist to keep it there. So he started giving her three fingers as she locked her knees together and tongued him. He returned the favor. It must have been a novelty to Juanita to be kissed so friendly in broad daylight, for it made her come again. He kept teasing her with his hand as he layed Ynez, his own climax delayed by the distraction, nice as it was. It was hard to stay in rhythm with two totally different bodies under him, bouncing out of step with one another. Juanita twisted her face away, gasping, "Enough! Have mercy I am too sensitized to stand it! Is not Ynez enough for you, for now?"

Ynez was. She was coming again. He got fully aboard and opened his eyes to see a pretty little face smiling up at him, heavy lidded with desire, and somehow it didn't matter that everything between pretty face and lovely lap was closer to the ground than Juanita's padded curves. He reached down to raise her thighs, cupping her silly looking buttocks in his palms to finish at a deeper angle. She sobbed in mingled pleasure and alarm as he started hitting bottom with every stroke while he played with what felt like a nice set of tits, shifted to the wrong part of her anatomy. She bit her lower lip and closed her eyes to climax, clamping down hard on his shaft as it exploded against her womb. She gasped and said, "Oh, you were right, Juanita. He is muy toro, and a sex maniac as well!"

Captain Gringo thought that was hardly fair, considering who'd started this orgy. But now that he was warmed up, he meant to finish it. So he threw the covers off and said, "All right, now that we've gotten the foreplay out of the way, let's get down to some serious fucking."

They left the campsite near the pyramid at dusk, well fed and rested. Or, at any rate, having spent most of the day off their feet. Juanita and Ynez wanted to march arm-in-arm with him along barely visible buried roadway. But he told them he couldn't shoot very good that way and sent them back to march with the other women as he and Gaston took the lead.

Had it been a regular military unit, Captain Gringo as the leader would not of course been out on point. But after talking to the surviving men just before sundown, after catching maybe four hours sleep between the two cozy adelitas, he'd discovered he'd been all too right about the guys he still had with him. The night attack had knocked off most of the men in the guerrilla who'd actually seen some fire fights as soldados or outlaws. He'd have to spend the next few rest stops whipping the outfit into shape. If any of the adelitas could fight with the enthusiasm they showed in other matters, things might work out. He knew he couldn't command, scout, and man the machinegun all at once. Maybe he'd show his two adelitas how to work the Maxim. Juanita was strong enough to be the ammo-packer and loader. Ynez had the better aim. He'd noticed people who aimed anything from a pool cue to a pussy well-tended to make natural sharpshooters.

The tropic moon looked close enough to reach up and

touch, so the savanna was well illuminated. If anything, the silvery sheen on the grass made the long-abandoned Mayan roadway even easier to follow. There were a few anxious moments when clumps of trees crowded in close, for the moonlight wasn't that bright and inky shadows could hold any number of dismal surprises. But apparently whoever used the shrine atop the pyramid for grim rites didn't know they were in the neighborhood, yet.

Walking at Captain Gringo's side, Gaston observed, "I have been wondering about the native drums, Dick?"

"What are you talking about? I don't hear any fucking drums."

"Exactly. That is what I have been wondering about. There were no throbbing tom-toms before they hit us last night, either."

Captain Gringo snorted and said. "Why should there have been? Geronimo never told us he was coming, either. I told you I've been boning up on the Maya, Gaston. Stop thinking of them as primitive Indians like we met down in Amazonia. In their day, they were, as civilized as the ancient Egyptians."

"*Merde alors*! Do you consider filling the cups of one's gods with human blood a civilized habit, Dick?"

"No. On religious matters they were pretty nasty. But lots of people who can read and write can be nasty about religious matters, Gaston. The Phoenicians went in for temple prostitution and fed babies, alive, to Moloch. Right now the secret police are killing Jews in the name of the Prince of Peace. Religion and civilization don't always mesh too well. Anyhow, the Maya had a regular army and military schools. It was a while back, of course, but the guys who hit us last night were pretty good. Give them repeating rifles instead of those spear casters and I'd match 'em against the average army in these parts."

"You have no idea how much that cheers me up, Dick! What if the next bunch we run into *has* guns?"

"We're in trouble, even if they only come at us with spears and those cricket bats with stone teeth! I hate to admit it when you're right, but this expedition isn't going well. I've been trying to figure out why the hell we were sent on it."

"Now you are starting to make sense! When do we desert?"

"We don't . . . we can't. Aside from the people depending on us, there's no place to go but forward. If we go back to Puerto Barrios as failures, Major Llamas might pay us off with bullets instead of a bonus. If we head for the coast, which doesn't sound much easier, when you consider it's a long hike through just as much trouble, we'd just be jumping from the frying pan into the fire. We'd arrive in Belize as two penniless and ragged strangers with a price on both our heads, and the British cops are better than most down here."

"Eh bien, but if we head due north, we'll be in Campeche, non?"

The tall American snorted in disgust and asked, "Haven't you seen enough of Mexico, Gaston? Los Rurales are meaner cops than the British Colonial Constabulary, and El Presidente Diaz is still sticking pins in our image every night before he goes to bed, I imagine."

"Ah, true, I'd forgotten about all the trains we wrecked the last time we were in Mexico. I wish I had your knack of making friends in high places, Dick. But, assuming we are not wiped out by Maya before we even find them, those mahogany pirates sound tough, too!"

"Yeah. We'll worry about that when we find them. They don't grow mahogany around here, so pick 'em up and lay 'em down."

They marched through the night, falling out for rest stops once an hour, but forbidden to light flares. He warned his followers that the human eye can spot a match flare as far as the horizon at night. So if they had to smoke, to pretend it was raining and keep everything

115

on fire cupped in their hands, adding that if he spotted any flares, he'd whip their asses without waiting to see if anyone else did.

His two adelitas kept suggesting sex each time they stopped, and it was tempting, since it was cool and they both looked better in the moonlight. But he said they had a day holed up in some trees ahead of them. So they should save it up for later. Nobody could sleep from sunrise to sunset, but he wanted to lie doggo by day and march at night as long as this open country held out.

It didn't. As the sun popped over the horizon with the sudden green flash of a tropic dawn, he saw the road they were following was leading them toward a wall of trees. The soil ahead had to be deeper. None of the brushy hammocks around them looked big enough to hide the whole band, if he and the girls wanted any privacy. So he decided to keep going. Once under cover of more jungle, there was no reason to stop until it got hotter later in the day. Naturally, Gaston protested, and naturally Captain Gringo told him to shut up, adding, "I got laid yesterday afternoon, too."

Gaston frowned and asked, "Who told you? That black girl and I were *très* discreet, I thought."

"I know the one you mean," Captain Gringo laughed. "Nice. But you only managed one?"

"*Merde alors*, at my age, one was enough. Lolita is *très* passionate, and bigger than me as well! But seriously, do we have to plunge headlong into that ominous-looking jungle ahead?"

"It's not half as ominous as being caught out here in the open. The buried slabs of this old Mayan road will have discouraged anything big from growing over it, so we'll have a path to follow, knowing it's headed the right way and, once we're under the canopy, the odds will be more even."

"Unless someone else knows about this road and has set up an ambush."

116

Captain Gringo shook his head and said, "You're not thinking. You've got that black girl, instead of soldiering, on your mind. Once we're under the canopy we'll be able to see between the trees in all directions. If we see a pile of brush, we'll know it shouldn't be there, and smoke it up. If I were a local, aiming to ambush anyone along this road, I'd have set up in one of the hammocks we've been passing all night."

Gaston shrugged and said, "True, but how many Maya have gone to West Point, hein?"

Captain Gringo didn't answer. He stopped and was shielding his eyes from the morning sun as he peered hard at what he'd just spotted closer to the trees. Gaston asked, "What is it? You are taller than me and can see farther."

The American took his hand from his eyes and raised it to halt the column in place as he told Gaston, "It looks like a cluster of buildings. Low, rambling, with white stucco and red-tile roofs."

"Ah, I see them now. I thought Maya favored thatched roofing, Dick"

"They do. They did even in Imperial times. The common Maya always lived in little grass huts, despite the grandeous architecture of the ruling class. Maybe that's why they don't have a ruling class these days. I'd say what we have up ahead is a hacienda, built by our kind of folks."

"Not *my* kind, Dick! No civilized Frenchman would be living out here in the middle of nowhere among wild Indians!"

"Come to think of it, I don't see Connecticut Yankees doing it, either. We're not going to find out standing here. We'll leave our people here and go in to see what they have to say for themselves."

"Can't we just go around? I don't like the looks of that mysterous place, Dick."

Captain Gringo shook his head and said, "Too late. They've spotted us and we must look mysterious to them, too, they're just moving the livestock in for exercise. We'd better go in before they come out. They probably think we're bandits, and anybody who can afford tile roofing can afford *guns*! So let's see if we can do it the friendly way.

They could, it seemed, after some confusion at first.

Leaving the outfit out on the savannah, well out of rifle range, the two soldiers of fortune strode to within pistol and shouting range and stopped, warily, to see what came next. What came next was a trio of guys on horseback. It was only a few yards to ride, but the guys on horseback must have thought it looked more impressive.

The one on the white horse looked impressive indeed as he sat atop his silver mounted saddle in a silver mounted charro outfit and big black sombero embroidered with silver thread. As Captain Gringo raised one hand in the universal gesture of good intentions, the leader on the white horse reined in, raised his own free hand, and called out, "I am Don Fernando Vallejo Martinez y Gomez-Perdenales and, with all due respect, señores, you are on my land."

"Sorry about that, Don Fernando," Captain Gringo said. "You don't seem to be on our government survey map. Repeat government! We're on a mission for the Guatemalan army. Want to see our papers?"

"*Me casa es su casa, señores.* I do not need to read your papers to see you are not Indians, and no bandits would be mad enough to trifle with *me*! Come, you can tell me all about it inside, where we shall be more comfortable, eh?"

"Thank you, Don Fernando. What about my people?"

"Your peons will be entertained by my peons, of course. I can see you both are caballeros. So if you will follow us, the main house, as you see, is not far."

He whirled his show horse around and headed back as his two mounted guards hesitated, saw neither Captain Gringo nor Gaston seemed to be shooting their boss in the ass from behind, and fell in on their flanks as Captain Gringo waved his followers in to follow, asking Gaston in softly murmured English, "How do you like it so far?"

Gaston shrugged and said, "I don't see why they'd want blood on their flooring, when they had us out here in the open to begin with. He's a bit imperious, but that goes with being a Don, one supposes. We'll probably make it if he doesn't catch us stealing the silver."

As they approached the arcade running along the front of the main house, a peon boy ran out to take the reins of Don Fernando's white horse as he got down. Once he was on the ground, they saw he was even shorter than Gaston in his high heels. That explained his Don Quixote act a lot.

The two soldiers of fortune exchanged glances. Gaston said he'd stay with the little people for now and see that they were all right. He didn't mention the machinegun, bless his heart.

The shrimpy local cock-of-the-walk shrugged and led Captain Gringo into the house. As soon as they were alone in a dark feudal hall, he removed his hat and murmured, "Forgive my arrogant behavior just now, señor. When one is short and bald it is most difficult to keep one's underlings in their places. My *vaqueros* are uncouth, and that Miguelito in particular is becoming difficult to keep in line."

Captain Gringo smiled and said, "You're not as short as they say Napoleon was, and they say bald men are very virile. Which one was Miguelito, the baby-faced one on the chestnut barb?"

"Yes. You are most simpatico for such a young good-looking man. But come, I shall introduce you to my wife and our other guests. You did not say why the government sent you, but you and your people will make a most welcome addition to our little garrison."

As he followed Don Fernando through an archway, Captain Gringo muttered something about running a survey to check the map of the area. Don Fernando wasn't on the map and he meant to know him better before he told him much. He asked what he meant about a garrison. Don Fernando said, "Indian trouble. I can see they were afraid to take on such a large party as your own, but we have had a devil of a time with them for the past few weeks."

By now they were entering a cavernous room where others sat around a table before a cold baronial fireplace. It was cold enough at night, one supposed, to need a fireplace. Meanwhile, it gave Don Fernando a nifty place to show off his elaborate family coat of arms.

The others rose as he and the hidalgo entered. Captain Gringo wasn't used to ladies rising when he entered a room, but he didn't have a family coat of arms. The others consisted of a pretty, plump little Castilian brunette, only an inch taller than her husband, and an English couple named Neville, both tall and blond. They looked more like brother and sister than man and wife, but it couldn't be helped. The country squires tended to marry cousins and, in the Nevilles' case, the inbreeding was starting to show. Cedric Neville was one of those tall, dishwater-blond drinks-of-water who never stood up straight and had a slight speech impediment. His wife, Pamela, looked like she had more sense, but she was a tall, dishwater-blond drink-of-water, too. Her face was passable, but her figure looked like what you'd get if you stood an ironing board up with two grapefruit halves pasted on it. As they all sat down and Doña Carmen rang for refreshments Don Fernando explained that the Nevilles were more usually to be found exploring Mayan ruins. Cedric, *Sir* Cedric as it turned out, but it was okay to call him Cedric, was "mucking about," as he put it, for the British Museum. Captain Gringo didn't ask him if he had a permit from the Guatemalan authorities. If he'd had, Major Llamas would have known he was here.

A pretty servant girl in a French maid's uniform and bare feet brought in a tray of glasses and a pitcher of sangria. As Don Carmen poured, the Englishman explained that he and his wife had staggered into the hacienda a jump ahead of some "bloody natives chucking spears." His wife shushed him with a look and took up the narration to explain they'd just found some lovely ruins not far away when they were attacked by truculent Indians and just made it after losing some porters and baggage.

Don Fernando nodded and said, "Fortunately, my own well-armed men were able to salvage most of the expedition's supplies and bring them here. Ocelot Who Dances doesn't like to face armed men in broad daylight."

Captain Gringo asked who Ocelot Who Dances was and the hidalgo explained that some friendly Maya had told him the young *Batabob* or Mayan chief had taken to killing people of late for reasons only an Indian could fathom.

Captain Gringo frowned and asked, "Are we talking about one band of about thirty guys, led by a muscular type wearing lots of green feathers?"

Don Fernando nodded and said that was a perfect description, adding, "Did you and your people run across him, then?"

Captain Gringo said, "I guess he ran across us. It was a pretty nasty fight, but guess who won? You don't have to worry about Ocelot Who Dances anymore, Don Fernando. We buried him and the other thirty-odd on the far side of that river to the south-west."

"My God," Don Fernando gasped, "you really are most welcome to my casa!" And Sir Cedric added, "I thay, good show, Yank. Now mayhaps we can get back to work on the cenothe I discovered!"

Captain Gringo had no idea what a "cenothe" might be and didn't want to. He said, "I guess it's safe, now. Did you people come in via British Honduras?"

"Of course. We started our digging over that way, but the ruins to the east have been picked over by earlier expeditions. You thee, Pam and I are trying to prove that Kukulcan was a Celtic Murdoch."

Captain Gringo sipped his drink and tried not to show how much that interested him. Lady Pamela must have been used to the effect her husband had on grown men. She shushed him again and said, "Murdoch, in the Gaelic, means something like a Viking. The pre-Christian Celts of the dark ages went in for sea raiding, too. The Maya's feathered serpent, Kukulkan, had a name that sounded very much like Cuchulain, the folk hero of Ulster. A dragon ship, carrying well armed murdochs would have seemed very impressive to Indians living in the savage state they were about three hundred A.D. The ruins here in this unexplored part of Guatemala are among the oldest. So we're looking for carvings that might show Kukulkan as a hero-god *in* a feathered serpent, not the feathered serpent himself."

Her husband cut in, enthusiastically, "Yeth! The *feathers* would have been the *sails,* you thee! After Kukulcan-Quetzalcoatl taught the ruddy buggers how to read and write and organize an army, he sailed back out to sea, according to the legends. He promised the Indians he'd return thomeday. So when Cortez arrived in sailing ships . . . "

Don Fernando's eyes were glazed, too. He said, "I can see all this is most important, Don Cedric. But if we can get back to *this* century, for a moment, we were discussing how safe the countryside might be, now that Señor Walker has wiped out the band we were having so much trouble with!"

Captain Gringo said, "Nobody's going to have trouble with that particular bunch, Don Fernando. Have you heard of other batabobs on the war path?"

The hidalgo shook his head but said, "Alas, the Maya I have working for me are all Cristiano. We never had trouble with the others, until recently. But apparently some priest of the old religion has been stirring things up. Naturally, friendly Maya of the true faith are not taken into the confidence of the pagans. However, rumor has it that Ocelot Who Dances was the main war chief. The *only* war chief, one hopes, no?"

"Well, we walked quite a ways without running into any others. It ought to be safe enough to work in daylight, for now. Just what sort of work do you do here, Don Fernando? I didnt see either standing crops or herds on the way in."

The hidalgo smiled and said, "My income comes from the jungle to the east, Señor Walker. I do not wish to *live* in the jungle, as I am neither an Indian nor an idiot. My peons work for me as chicleros, cruising the jungle for sapodilla trees."

"You mean, all this is supported by chewing gum?"

"We find this odd, too, but apparently a lot of people in your land chew gum. We send the raw chicle to a great plant in Chicago, where it is flavored and wrapped in tinfoil to ruin the teeth of Yanqui children."

"Gotcha. How do you get it to market from here, Don Fernando? I'm not being nosy. I'm working for your government. My map doesn't show any roads or waterways around here."

Don Fernando nodded and said, "There is nothing one could call a *road*. That is why I am so pleased about you killing those Mayan raiders. When we have a shipment to send, it goes through the jungle to the British port of Belize. There is no road worth putting on any map, but my mules get through with the chicle, when nobody casts spears at them."

Cedric Neville nodded and said, "Narrow ruddy path, actually. Pam and me followed it west from the Honduran ruins."

124

Captain Gringo took out his map and handed it to the Englishman, saying, "I wonder if you'd take a look at this. It hasn't been agreeing at all with the things I keep finding in this neck of the woods."

Sir Cedric took the map, but Lady Pamela took it from him, made room on the table for it, and spread it out. She frowned down at it for a few moments before she said, "This is all wrong, Mister Walker. It doesn't agree at all with *our* map, and our map is British!"

"I'm sure that makes all the difference in the world. What's wrong with my map, Lady Pamela?"

"Everything. Call me Pam. You have some silly rivers that don't exist, for one thing. You're missing the Rio Hondo, too. Can't for the life of me see how anyone who'd ever been in these parts could miss the Rio Hondo!"

"I guess the cartographer needed the job, Pam. Where's this Rio Hondo supposed to be?"

She traced a line with her fingernail as she answered, "Roughly along about here. If I can take this to my room during the coming siesta I'll trace it off our British survey map for you."

He nodded in agreement as he watched her nail run north and then cut east north-east near the Mexican border to aim for the Atlantic as she said, "The river forms the border between British Honduras and the Mexican State of Quintana Roo. Can't see how even a *Guatemalan* cartographer could have missed *that*!"

Captain Gringo couldn't either. Now that he looked closer, the border line did meander sort like a water course, but it wasn't labeled a Rio anything, and the inland headwaters weren't on the map at all. He said, "If I wanted to float east to the coast, would the Rio Hondo be my best bet, Pam?"

She frowned and said, "Not if you wanted to end up anywhere important. The Hondo ends in a coastal mangrove swamp. Why not float down the Rio Belize itself? Its headwaters start only a little south of here."

He frowned, staring down at the blank paper her nail was now pointing to, and asked, "Rio Belize, Pam?"

"Of course, Dick. How did you think the port of Belize got it's name? It's the only river that runs as far inland as Guatemala from our sea port on the coast."

He turned to stare at Don Fernando as he asked, "And you use a path?"

The hidalgo looked blank. Then he smiled and said, "Ah, I see what you mean. The Rio Belize is not suited for paddling down in a canoe, señor. It is mostly rapids. It is true some loggers float their timber down to Belize via the river. My chicle bales, alas, do not float well."

That sounded reasonable. But why wasn't such an obvious route for the pirated mahogany on his fucking map? He asked, "Does anybody live along the Rio Belize?" Don Fernando nodded and agreed, "Sí. The main source of the Belize starts near the town of San Lorenzo. As the river crosses the border, it passes between the towns of Cayo and Buengue Viejo."

"Any border guards there, Don Fernando?"

"Of course, there are both British and Guatemalan customs officers, just as to the north at Yaloch."

Captain Gringo nodded, keeping some of what he was thinking to himself. He wouldn't know for sure until Pamela Neville reworked his stupid map, but it was beginning to look like the purloined mahogany really had to be crossing the line near Naranjo. The invisible but apparently well-known passes traced by Pam's nails were about fifty miles apart, with the ruins of Naranjo about in the middle. Once the logs were safely in British Honduras, they were obviously being rafted innocently to Port Belize as if they'd been cut legally. He asked the company at large if they knew any other streams between the Hondo and the Belize. They all agreed there weren't any and that a low limestone ridge to the east made it seem unlikely. So that was that. How far could a gang of guys pick up and move a mahogany log, if they really wanted to? Not far. There had to be a way not even the locals knew of.

He wasn't about to find it here. But it was getting on to siesta time and good old Pam had said she'd draw some sense on his map, so what the hell. He'd rest his people and his own ass, and they'd be on their way later in the day, when the tropic sun got a bit more reasonable.

He settled back and took out a cigar as he shot an inquiring glance at the lady of the house. Doña Carmen hadn't said a word since they'd been introduced. The conversation had been carried on in English and might have been over her head. But she dimpled at him and nodded, so he lit his smoke. She dimpled nicely. It seemed such a waste that she'd be spending La Siesta with her even shorter and plumper little hubby. He tried not to picture two Kewpie dolls going sixty-nine, but it wasn't easy. He'd told Juanita and Ynez to expect another orgy during the coming siesta, and they were going to be mad as hell about him spending it alone here in the house, too. He blew a smoke ring and tried to picture the Nevilles in bed together. That did wonders for his dawning erection. As he smiled politely at them, the thought of either of them, naked, was horrible to contemplate. Sir Cedric was droning on about his Goddamn Celtic sea rover and his Goddamn nearby ruins around his Goddamn "cenothe." And then, as the Englishman said something about throwing virgins in the water, Captain Gringo sat up straighter as the penny dropped. *His* book on the Maya called those big wells *cenotes*, but that was close enough. He asked Sir Cedric, "Wait a minute, Cedric. Are you talking about one of those big water-filled craters in the limestone bedrock?"

Sir Cedric nodded and said, "Of courth. They're a natural land form in this sort of limestone country, dear Boy. The Maya theemed to think their god, Xoc, enjoyed a helping of virgin now and again during the dry theason. Loaded the poor dears with gold and jade and chucked them in the deep cenothe to drown. We'd salvaged thome jade and a spot of gold before we were attacked. Going back there, now, and dive some more, eh what?"

Captain Gringo wasn't interested in virgins dead a thousand years. But he remembered something else about karst topgraphy, now! He snapped his fingers and said, "Those well-like openings in the surface are the sink holes into underground limestone caves! Meaning that if the one you found is full of water, this late in the dry season, there's an underground river down there! You said something about diving . . . ?"

Sir Cedric nodded and said, "Yeth. We left a diving suit behind when the Maya started chucking spears at us. Hope they didn't spear it. Set up, the diving suit lookth thort of like a perthonage, eh what?"

Military plans were meant to be changed. Captain Gringo grinned as he smoked on—things were looking up at last. If Major Llamas wasn't just trying to get them killed, as Gaston suggested, he'd responded to vague rumors about mahogany pirates by hastily scraping together an expedition of expendables, given them a vague map, and threw them in the general direction of the annoyance the way a housewife throws water at an alley cat yowling under her window and keeping her awake. The pencil pushing major probably didn't expect them to solve his problem, but it kept him behind his comfortable desk instead of ducking spears or bullets in all this heat.

But with Pam's help he'd wind up with a decent map. And if he could check the current in that underground river, and it went either north or south, the problem was half solved. The illicit loggers were dropping the mahogany into a cenote. Not the one the Nevilles had been exploring, of course. Another one. Sink holes came in bunches in limestone karstlands. If they all dropped into one underground river, the mahogany pirates could use the nearest one handy. The mahogany grew in the jungle above the caverns. If there was much of a current, the logs would all go the same way until the natural drainage popped them out on the open water of either the Hondo or Belize. Confederates there, well inside the Honduran border, could raft them together and float them down to the coast as legal logs!

He was betting on the Rio Belize, since the nasty skipper of the *Imperial Trader* was waiting for a load there. But he had to be sure before he made his next move. Once he knew which way the underground current ran, he'd head down the right river with his guerrillas, looking for cave openings in the banks. They'd been told to do their fighting on the Guatemalan side of the border, but why fuck around? What London and Guatemala City didn't know wouldn't hurt them. It could take forever rounding up scattered logging gangs in the jungle running fifty miles along the border. They'd stop logging pronto, once there was no way to get the heavy mahogany out. The guys set up well inside British Honduras wouldn't be expecting an attack, either. Yeah, the more he thought about it, the more he liked it. He hoped the skipper or at least some officers off the *Imperial Trader* would be waiting at the receiving end of the underground river. They owed him.

By siesta time, Captain Gringo already felt rested and 'as full of more sangria than he'd really needed. But no matter how one felt in the tropics, he didn't wander about in the noonday sun. So he followed the maid Don Fernando told him to and she led him to a second-story room. She wasn't the one who'd been sloshing sangria at them. But she was even prettier. He could see as he followed her up the stairs that she saw no need for a corset, or anything else, under the thin, black poplin uniform.

Alas, after she'd shown him into the guest room, she left him there alone. The big four-poster in one corner looked comfortable, but what the hell did a guy need with a bed—alone—in the middle of the day?

The jalousied blinds were closed, of course, so the room, while cool, was darkish. He moved a chair over by the window and cracked open the slats for more light as he read more on the ancient Maya and their underwater gods. He wanted to sound intelligent when he accompanied the Nevilles to the cenote they were exploring a few miles away.

As he adjusted the blinds, he spotted movement in the courtyard below. Anybody moving in the open during La Siesta had to be up to something he thought was important, and you could see from here that the vaquero, Miguelito, was walking sneaky.

The good-looking peon moved into the shadows of the main house and looked around to see if he was being observed. He was, but he couldn't see Captain Gringo peeking through the jalousies at him. Miguelito assumed the coast was clear and started climbing a thick vine growing up the side of the house. Captain Gringo wondered if burglary was any of his business. Then the blinds of the window Miguelito was climbing toward opened and the watching American saw Miguelito wasn't a burglar. Doña Carmen, stark naked, smiled down at Miguelito over her heroic creamy breasts. The gallant Miguelito put his back into it and finished his climb posthaste and doubtless with a hard-on. He forked a leg over the sill and took his host's wife in his arms and then, just as it was getting interesting, the son-of-a-bitch closed the blinds and Captain Gringo had to guess the rest.

The only mystery was where the hell Don Fernando was spending his own siesta while all this going on. Captain Gringo sighed, "Oh, yeah, both the maids were nice-looking."

He sat down with a weary chuckle, glad he wasn't married. He probably would have been, by now, if they hadn't tried to hang him on that false charge back in the States and launched him on a wilder career. He wondered if he'd have cheated on any gal he'd married, once the honeymoon was over and sleeping with the same woman night after night got down to being just another chore, like winding the clock or putting out the cat.

Doña Carmen was a pretty little thing, as Miguelito no doubt thought, too. But she and Don Fernando had apparently been married some time and, what the hell, there wasn't much *else* to do out here in the middle of no place! The climate probably had a lot to do with the people screwing like mink down here. The heat made everyone dress light enough to be noticed by the opposite sex and the long siestas provided a lot of private hours of temptation.

There wasn't anything he didn't already know about

cenotes in the damned little book. The Mayan gods demanded all sorts of nasty rites. When they hadn't been filling bowls with blood, the Mayan priests had liked to fill the big natural wells with drowned corpses. Just why the god, Xoc, insisted on virgins wasn't clear. Maybe like most religious fanatics, the Mayan priests were undersexed and didn't want the other guys to have any fun.

From across the room there was a discreet tap on the door. Thinking it was Pam, Captain Gringo put the book aside and went to let her in, hoping she'd finished the map.

But it was her husband, Cedric. He was wearing a terry cloth bathrobe and he'd switched to something stronger than sangria, from the glassy look in his eye. As he came in, he said, "I've been longing to get you alone, Dear Boy."

Captain Gringo felt uneasy about the way the skinny Englishman was batting his eyes, so he said, "I was expecting your wife. I mean, expecting her to bring that map back, of course."

"Oh, she'll be on it at least an hour, knowing how thorough poor Pam is."

He wasn't lisping, now. Apparently he felt more sure of himself with a pint or so of booze in him. He looked around, saw the bed, and said, "Oh, yummy" and walked toward it, peeling off his bathrobe.

Captain Gringo stared at the awful naked body of the silly twit and asked, "Cedric, just what the fuck are you doing?"

By the bed Sir Cedric turned to face him, his pecker about the size of a twelve-year-old boy's. But it was standing fully erect as he simpered, "Fucking is exactly what I had in mind."

Then he turned again, climbed on the bed on hands and knees, and arched his spine to present his open buttocks to the startled Captain Gringo as he purred, "You can see I've already greased my arse. Come over here and show it hard. I'm just dying to be fucked!"

Captain Gringo grimaced and said, "Gee, Cedric, I hate to have to be the one to tell you this, but I'm queer."

"Oh, I *knew* you'd been to a good school! I was hoping you were queer!"

"I meant I'm queer from *your* point of view, pal. I've got this funny sexual hangup I can't do anything about."

Cedric wiggled his rump as he smiled back archly over one shoulder to say, "Oh, marvelous! Tell me what sort of perversions you prefer, Dear Boy. You'll find me game, for almost anything. What do you want to do to me?"

"Nothing. You see, I'm queer for women. I've fought it all my life, but it's no use, Cedric. I just can't keep from wanting to screw dames."

The Englishman flinched and rolled over to sit up, primly, as he asked, severely, "Are you saying you're rejecting me, you brute?"

"I'm afraid so, Cedric. I'd like to help you out, as a pal, but I'm just not up to it."

"What if I sucked you first? I'll bet I could get it up for you that way."

"No thanks. I'm just not interested in sex with another guy."

Cedric looked hurt and asked, "What if I was more attractive? Haven't you ever met a man who aroused your interest, Dick?"

"Not that kind of interest."

"What would you do if you *did* meet a man, or say a very attractive boy, who aroused you sexually, Dick?"

"Gee, I don't know. It's never come up. I guess if I wanted to make love to a male, I would. I've never been shy about screwing anybody that appealed to me. But you're just not my type. Sorry about that."

Sir Cedric bent down to pick up his robe as he said with a sigh, "I see you're one of those invincible, born heteros. At least you didn't want to beat me up. Are we still friends, Dick?"

As the disappointed fellow rose, Captain Gringo held out a hand to shake as he said, "Sure. I've made many a pass at a gal who wanted to keep it platonic, Cedric. What just happened wasn't your fault or mine. It was just a natural difference of opinion. Later this afternoon, will you show me around that cenote you're working on?"

Sir Cedric shook his hand with an embarrassed smile and said he'd be pleased as punch, so they parted friendly, if not the kind of friends old Cedric had in mind.

Captain Gringo shut the door after him and moved over to the window to see if anyone else was going nuts around here. This siesta was a pisser. Doña Carmen was just down the hall balling the jack with Miguelito. Don Fernando was screwing the hired help. Gaston was probably tearing off some stuff with that great looking black adelita, and he was feeling sort of left out.

Damn the caste system here. He had two great-looking broads, or, well, *one* great-looking broad if you put Juanita's torso between the face and snatch of Ynez, and they expected him to spend the next three hours or so *alone* up here!

There was another knock on the door. He went to open it cautiously, hoping Sir Cedric wasn't demanding a rematch. But is was his wife, Lady Pamela. She was wearing the same terry cloth robe, or one that matched her husband's. She came in, sounding oddly breathless, as she handed him his old map and said, "I made all the changes in waterproof India ink, Dick."

He said, "Thanks," then shut the door behind her, picked her up, and carried her over to the bed. As he lowered her onto the mattress and began to unwrap her, she asked, conversationally, "I say, are you always so forward, Dick?" But he noticed she didn't resist as he opened her robe, put a hand on one of her naked breasts, and leaned over to kiss her.

He'd been right about her body. She was lean and hard everywhere she wasn't tit, above the waist. Her face was okay, and she kissed back very nicely as she took him in her arms. He ran an exploratory hand down her skinny flank and saw the gathered folds of her skirts had been hiding a pair of hips that went with the other good parts. As he cupped her blond privates in his palm and parted the hair with a probing finger, she whispered, her lips on his, "Oh, very well, but aren't you going to take your clothes off, first?"

He laughed and let her go as he sat up to take his shirt and pants off. Pam wriggled out of the robe with a smile and said, "My God, those shoulders are real. I thought it was padding." Then, as he stood up to shuck his pants, she gasped, "Good God! Be careful where you aim that thing! I'm not used to such a monstrous weapon!"

Somehow, this came as no great surprise to Captain Gringo. But he didn't tell her how he knew what kind of screwing she'd been getting lately, if any at all.

As he mounted her with no further preliminaries and, as she welcomed him with open arms and thighs, he knew he'd been right about her showing up at his door in just her bathrobe. She must have been related to her husband, for she was built like a twelve-year-old down there, too. He'd have felt like a child molester if her tight, little vagina hadn't come with a rather horsey and love-starved big blond.

"Oh, Jesus," she gasped. "I've never felt anything like that in me before!" But apparently it didn't bother her to be fully opened up, from the way she was moving her hips in time with his thrusts. They were both excited to begin with, so they came fast, together, with Pam's long and surprisingly shapely legs wrapped tightly around his waist. She held him so, sobbing, as they both went limp. She murmured, "I'm glad you didn't muck about with the usual gallantries. I suppose you think I'm dreadful?"

He moved inside her, teasingly, as he soothed, "I think you're swell. I really needed that."

"Oh, so did I. If you only knew," she replied wistfully, but to her credit, she was too loyal to her husband to say

135

why. Instead, she added "I do feel low, cheating on poor Cedric with another man. But his work keeps him so busy and . . . "

"Hey, if you don't want to feel low, why don't you get on top?"

"Good Lord? Do you mean we can do it again?"

"Sure. Doesn't everybody?"

She didn't answer as he rolled off to let her mount him, wearing a Mona Lisa expression. She seemed a lot prettier, up here, now that she'd literally let her hair down. As she leaned forward to impale herself on his erection, her long blond hair hung down over her breasts so that they played peek-a-boo with him as she started bouncing, saying, "I say, this does feel jolly good. It's rather like posting a horse, with the pommel in a rather naughty position. We don't have horns like this on English saddles, of course. It feels like . . ." and then she dropped her upper class act and sobbed, "Oh, Darling, I'm so happy!" as she proceeded to go crazy with him.

It was a long siesta, so he went a little crazy, too. He figured she had it coming. She was a nice old gal and it was a shame she'd gotten this far along in life without really being used and abused properly by a real man. So he gave it to her in every position but flying and he'd have tried that if they'd had wings. The contrast between her big-boned lean and blond body and the last few women he'd had was stimulating enough. Her hungry little love maw was so tight he couldn't have gone soft if he'd wanted to. But after a while, as he was slamming her dog style, his back started to give out. So when she came and fell forward across the bed he just flopped beside her, taking her in his arms to comfort her and get his breath back. She snuggled her fluffed blond head against his chest, kissing one of his nipples as she purred, "Oh, God, if only this never had to end. I could go on like this forever, Dick."

"Forever is a fib, Pam."

"I know—I'm a married woman. You may think this

sounds crazy, but I have no intention of leaving my husband for you, Darling."

He tried to keep a straight face as he kissed the part in her hair to murmur, "I know. Stiff upper lip and all that. We'll have to be civilized about all this, eh what?"

"Don't mock me, Dick. I really feel dreadful about having to leave you, for now. But I must get back to Cedric before he becomes suspicious. I told him I was coming here, of course, but the way I came indeed must remain our little secret. Do I have your word you'll be discreet?"

"Hell, who am I to tell about it, for God's sake?"

"Some men do, you know. I've only done this sort of thing a few times, and never with anyone as nice. But I had a dreadful time of it when a man I trusted back in England kissed and told at his club."

"He must have been a bounder."

"He was. Fortunately, for some reason Cedric thought he was a fairy, so he didn't believe the gossip. I'd die if he found out about us!"

Captain Gringo knew she was having second thoughts, so that meant she'd been screwed enough. He patted her and said, "Mum's the word, Pam. Uh, when are we going to get together like this again?"

"Do you still want to? Didn't I satisfy you, Darling?"

"Hell yes! But tomorrow is another day."

She sat up and started to put her hair up again as she smiled down at him and said, "We'll worry about tomorrow when tomorrow comes. I think I rather enjoy the way you've been teaching me about coming."

Later that same afternoon everyone reassembled downstairs looking innocent as hell, considering. The Nevilles were anxious to go back to the cenote and find out if the Indians had wrecked the gear they'd been forced to leave behind. Captain Gringo was anxious about that sink hole, too. So when the Nevilles headed out into the jungle with some of their own workers, Captain Gringo, Gaston, and couple of his own gunhands tagged along. Don Fernando and his wife said they'd wait at the house. They both looked a little tired, considering they'd just gotten out of bed.

The cenote looked about like what Captain Gringo expected: a big steep-walled crater about two tennis courts across. The calm water maybe twenty feet below ground level was scummed with floating weed and as dark a shade of brown as sepia ink. Sir Cedric ignored the cenote to run around from one box and bale to another, checking the contents. The raiding Indians hadn't been out for anything but blood. Some of the equipment was scattered around, but nothing important had been stolen. A rubbersized canvas diving suit sat up like a brass-headed scarecrow near a hand-driven pumpbox, and it hadn't been touched at all. Sir Cedric explained it was propped up like that with a stick inside the helmet to keep the rubber from sticking together in the heat. The Indians must have seen it looked pretty spooky and decided they'd better not mess with it.

Captain Gringo joined him as Sir Cedric fiddled with the valves and seemed to find everything in order. The American nodded and responded, "Quite some rig, for archeology."

The Englishman shrugged, sweeping a negligent hand at the few blocks of white stone scattered in the nearby grass as he said, "Yeth, it was quite expensive, but you can thee there's nothing much to be found up here amid these picked-over ruins. Nobody leaves gold or jade about for a thousand years. But the decorations the sacrifices wore are still down there on the bottom, with their bones. Unfortunately, under a lot of muck. You'd be surprised how much thilt settles over things in a thousand years."

Captain Gringo nodded and said, "No I wouldn't. You say you've been down in the hole. Did you notice if there was any current under the surface?"

Sir Cedric nodded and answered, "Not what one could call a strong current, but I did notice the stirred up muck tended to drift off to one thide all the while. There's a sort of tunnel running off through one wall down there. I have no intention of exploring it, thank you. Nothing as heavy as I'm after would have drifted into the rather spooky thing. It looks rather dangerous besides."

"How come? Are there fish or crocodiles down there?"

"Lord, no. No way for them to get to thith isolated cenothe. The danger would be to the diver's air-line. Lifeline, too, for that matter Only a fool would drag a rubber hose and manila life-line under overhanging, jagged rock, eh what?"

Captain Gringo stared down at the diving suit and saw that since the Englishman was almost as tall as he, it should fit. He said, "I've been down in a hard hat. Do you have anything that lights up under water?"

"Of course. How did you think I found the few bits of

jewelry I brought up? We have chemical flares that burn under water. That box over there. I don't think the Indians knew what they were. Why?"

Captain Gringo looked up at the sky and said, "There's a couple of hours of light left. I'd like to borrow your diving suit and have a peek down that side tunnel. If it joins a stream that's moving better, we'll know these cenotes are all connected, underground."

Sir Cedric snorted and said, "You mean you will. I don't care if they do or don't. I'm an archeologist, not a flaming geologist!"

"Can I borrow the rig?"

The Englishman shrugged and said, "If you like. I'll get the lads who know how to fit one in and work the pump."

As he wandered off, Pamela, who'd been talking to Gaston, came over with Gaston to join Captain Gringo by the diving outfit. When he told them what was up, Gaston blanched and said, "Dick, you are *très* crazy! You are a machinegunner, not a deep sea diver!"

Pamela said, "He's right, Dick. It could be dangerous." But Captain Gringo shrugged and said, "What isn't? That's not a deep sea, Pam. It's only a mud puddle."

Pam said, soberly, "Dick, that mud puddle is over fifty-feet deep, and you're so right about the mud part! Cedric says it's pitch black near the bottom, if you can call it a bottom. It seems to consist of waterlogged sticks and thick goo. Despite his appearance, Cedric's a skilled diver, and he says it's dangerous down there. If you were to snag your line or cut your air hose on the sharp rock, how could anyone hope to save you? You'd be wearing the only diving suit between here and the coast!"

As Captain Gringo was shrugging that one off, Sir Cedric came back with his brownies. The Englishman repeated his wife's warnings but, meanwhile, the three of them got the tall American into the suit.

This was easier said than done. The only openings in the bulky man-shaped, rubberized bag were at the top where the brass helmet plate rested and at the ends of the

140

sleeves, where you could shove your bare hands out if you pushed like hell.

Captain Gringo tossed his jacket and sombrero aside before starting to wriggle in, of course. He thought about his shoulder holster and decided it was okay where it was. He didn't have a better place to leave his .38. With the two pumpmen helping, he got in *sans* helmet and stood up, saying, "Jesus, this is heavy," and Sir Cedric said, "Wait 'til you have the helmet on and the lead weights around your waist, Dear Boy. It's *supposed* to be heavy, to keep you on the perishing *bottom!*"

As the others helped with the remaining gear, he started clumping toward the cenote on the heavily-weighted shoes, leaving deep footprints. Sir Cedric said, "I thay, you are a brute! Most men can hardly walk in one of those thuits, out of the wather."

"You call this walking? I feel like a castiron duck."

Gaston laughed and opined, "*Merde alors,* you could haunt a house, Dick. Did you ever read that amusing novel by Miss Shelley, about Frankenstein? If they ever make it a stage play, you'll be perfect for the part."

By this time they were as close to the edge of the cenote as it was safe without the helmet. So Captain Gringo stopped and the pump men screwed it on and attached the air-hose. As Sir Cedric hooked the manila life-line to the belt, lifted it with a grunt, and fastened it around the canvas waist, the pumpers ran back and started cranking. It was about time. The inside of the suit smelled like used tennis shoes, even with air coming through the hose. Captain Gringo shouted to be heard through the thick-glass port-holes in front and one either side of the heavy helmet and when Sir Cedric gathered he was asking how they'd lower him into the cenote, he shouted back, "You just jump, Dear Boy. When you want to come up, yank once on the life-line. Two yankth mean you want more line."

Captain Gringo nodded, remembering the last time he'd messed around like this. Naturally, they didn't see him nod, so everyone was startled when he staggered forward and dropped over the edge to hit the water with a mighty splash and vanish beneath the dark surface.

The hose and life-line trailed after him over the edge as he kept going. So Sir Cedric yelled, "Pump harder to keep up the pressure, Lads. You there, Hernan, pick up the lines to keep them from chafing on the edge."

As Gaston joined the Englishman nearer the edge to stare down morosely at the bubbles rising to the surface like some giant cannibal pot coming to a boil, Sir Cedric said, "My, Dick theartenly ith impetuouth!"

Gaston sighed and replied, "He is inclined to move fast, once he makes up his mind about something."

Meanwhile, on the bottom, Captain Gringo was beginning to wonder if this had been such a hot idea after all. His booted feet seemed to be stuck in something nasty, half-way up his shins and he couldn't see a thing in the murky water. He took one of the underwater flares from his suit belt and felt with his fingers in the fetid water to make sure which end was which. Then, holding the flare in one hand, he pulled the friction string at the other and discovered you *could* have a flame under water if you mixed an oxident with the other goodies!

He stared like a kid with a new toy as the end of the wax paper torch burned a bright red in its private diving bell of bubbling steam. He could see all around for several yards. He hauled one boot out of the muck, braced it on a mass of water-logged wood, and got himself out of the mud. He leaned forward and walked in slow motion until he saw the steep limestone wall of the cenote and, sure enough, there seemed to be a cave-like opening ahead. As he ducked lower to enter it, he forgave Sir Cedric for a certain lack of curiosity. It looked pretty spooky. As he got under the overhang, he gathered his hose and life-line in his free hand to keep them from scraping on the overhang. The helmet bubbles and torch steam rose to the jagged roof to roll like quick-silver back the way he'd come. So he knew the tunnel was taking him deeper into the guts of Guatemala. There was a valve on the helmet he could use to increase or decrease pressure in the suit. But he left it alone for now. The slope didn't seem that steep. He saw it wasn't straight, either. He warily edged around a turn, holding the torch high. There was less silt on the stone floor than out in the open cenote, but there was enough to show that a slight current did in fact suck some of the crud this way. The tunnel opened into a bigger chamber and he froze in place, hair tingling inside the brass helmet, as he saw what lay ahead.

Some of the sacrificial victims of the ancient Mayan priests hadn't been weighted enough to keep them all the way down. A jumbled mass of skulls and bones were scattered on the tunnel floor, covered with brown moss and still haunted by the horror of mass death a thousand years before.

But the silt stirred up by his weighted boots was drifting faster as well as further down the tunnel. So he plowed on through, saying, "Excuse me" as he accidentally kicked a skull and sent it rolling ahead of him.

Up at ground level, the others of course were unaware of what he'd found, but worried just the same. Sir Cedric watched a mark on the life-line go under the scummy surface as he muttered, "I thay, where could he be going? He's trailing two hundred yards, now, and the perishing cenothe is only fifty feet deep!"

His wife shot an anxious glance at the sky and added, "It will be dark in about an hour, too. But not to worry. He's almost to the end of the lines now, so he'll have to turn back soon whether he wants to or not."

Gaston was only half listening as he watched the bubbles rising along the edge of the pool below. The exhaust of his comrade's air of course was bursting from the lip of the underwater tunnel. Or, at least, it had been! Gaston pointed and shouted, "*Regardez*! Dick's air has stopped! His hose must be kinked!"

Pam gasped. "Oh, my God!" and bent down to grab the life-line as she added, "Help me pull him out before he suffocates!" So Gaston did, and together they leaned back against the rope as Sir Cedric shouted something so screwed up they couldn't understand him. Then Gaston sat down, hard, with Pam in his lap, as they both stared stupefied at the limp line they were holding. Pam wailed, "Oh, no! The life-line's broken!"

Sir Cedric was jumping from one foot to the other like a kid trying not to wet his pants as he shouted, "Oh, you thilly! You cut his rope on the rocks!"

Gaston shoved Pam off him, rolled over, and grabbed the rubber hose, saying, "Eh bien, this won't cut as easily and if we pull *très* gentle . . . "

Then he tested the hose's resistance, pulled harder, and gagged. He could tell just by feeling that it wasn't attached to anything! He hauled in a couple of coils and now air was rising from the tunnel mouth again, but the hose obviously was no longer attached to Captain Gringo! Gaston shouted, "We must save him!" But Pam asked, white as a sheet as she got to her feet, "How, Gaston? He's fifty feet down and at least three hundred feet into that tunnel, in the only diving suit for hundreds of miles!"

"He's dead by now," added her husband, as Gaston kept hauling in rope and life-line. As the severed ends came over the rim of the cenote, Gaston gasped, "*Mon Dieu!* Look at that rope! It wasn't chaffed by the rocks! It was most obviously cut with a knife!"

Pam looked accusingly at her husband as she said, "Dick has a knife on his belt, but obviously *he* didn't cut it."

Sir Cedric blanched and said, "Don't look at me! How on earth could I have done it, and why on earth would I want to?"

"Never mind why you'd want to, you silly sod. If you can't stand rejection you should stick with your own kind. Let me see that rope, Gaston. It could have been cut part way, before Dick went down. We didn't lower him on the line, you know."

Gaston handed her the severed end, but sighed, "I'm

way ahead of you, Madame, but the three of us are inno-
cent. One can see the rope was cut with one good slash.
The mystery remaining is who could have done it, since
I, for one, do not believe in mermaids!"

Actually, the life-line had been cut by Captain Gringo himself, and even he had thought it was a lousy idea. But he'd had no choice.

In the tunnel the bubbles on the roof had suddenly started going the other way as the floor ahead, sloped upward and as his brass helmet suddenly rose above the surface in an air-filled cavern, the hose had snagged behind him and, apparently not being meant to hang at such an angle, popped off the nipple on the helmet to go snaking off like a rocket trailing high pressure bubbles. A few moments later he'd felt them trying to haul him back down the tunnel by the line attached to his harness, and that hadn't tickled his fancy much.

He knew if he was hauled under water with a gaping hole instead of an air-hose in the side of the helmet, he'd drown. So he'd done the only thing he could. He'd cut his life line. That, of course, left him standing in chest deep water, somewhere in a cave, with his torch burning down. He couldn't go back, so he staggered forward, the water level dropping around him. The suit was heavy as hell.

The current helped though. It was stronger now as it ran east under the surface. But the tunnel floor was still rising and the water was now knee deep. Could water run uphill?

As he rounded a bend, the mystery was answered. The tunnel forked. One passage led upward, exposing a dry albeit slimy-looking floor. The water ran over shallows that formed the lip of what sounded like an underground waterfall. He didn't want to go deeper. He wanted up. So he took the passage that seemed to head for the surface.

The torch was about shot. He dropped it, still sputtering, and lit another before he pressed on. The flare behind him cast his monstrous shadow ahead of him. He even looked spooky to himself. He had to get out of this fucking rubber union suit. But that was easier said than done. He felt the bolts of the helmet with his free hand. He had strong hands, but they weren't as strong as the wrenches Sir Cedric's helpers had used to lock him in this dumb diving suit! The face ports wouldn't open. He could breathe, thanks to the hole in the helmet, but he was already starting to sweat in the rubberized suit. As he followed the tunnel he saw that wherever it reached the surface, if it ever did, he'd be a long way from Gaston and the others and his fucking .38 was strapped to his ribs inside the suit!

The tunnel took another turn. He had a compass in his pocket, but he couldn't get to that, either, and he was starting to get turned-around down here.

There wasn't much he could do about it. The tunnel floor was now dry and his heavy boots stirred fine dust from the limestone underfoot. He started spotting sticks and leaf mold in the passage which meant it had to connect with the surface. But how the hell far did he have to walk in this stupid diving suit before he reached it? He snapped his fingers and cursed himself for not thinking. Then he unfastened the weight belt, keeping the diver's knife as he let it clunk to the floor. The suit was still too heavy for the average man to have walked in, but Captain Gringo wasn't an average man and getting rid of that extra weight helped a lot. If he didn't actually walk with a spring to his steps, at least he could walk.

The heavy boots clunked like horse's hooves on their

147

lead soles. So he thought, at first, he was hearing their echoes. But after he'd been blundering on for what seemed like a million years, he had to stop to light another torch, and that's when he noticed that something was still thumping.

He couldn't make out the direction of the drum-like sounds, but they could hardly be coming from behind him. It could be the people he'd left topside, trying to signal him. He had no idea how thick the limestone roof above him was. Maybe the local natives knew about this passage and were pounding up there to signal him? Sure they were. That's why they were beating like a tom-tom.

He moved on, toward the drum beats. He came to a steeper incline and as he staggered up it he saw two-headed dragons and long-nosed rain gods painted on the tunnel walls. That was something to think about. So he stopped to think. It wasn't easy. He was half-suffocated in the hot rubber suit and little stars were pinwheeling in his eyes from the effort of breathing through the one little hole in the brass bowl his head was locked into, like the "Man In The Iron Mask." He stuck the end of the torch in a crack to try an experiment. It worked. He couldn't get out, but he could pull his right hand inside the sleeve of the loose fitting diving suit. He grunted his arm all the way in, leaving the right sleeve to dangle and provide more air as he got to his revolver. Then holding the muzzle of the gun against the chest of the suit so it bulged like a big rubber tit, he tucked the knife under his left arm pit, yanked out the torch, and kept going. The empty flapping sleeve acted like a bellows and allowed the hot air in the suit to rise out the helmet hole. So his head began to clear a bit as he struggled up the incline, rounded a turn, and came face to face with a blank wall. Some sons-of-bitches had walled the tunnel with stone blocks!

He could hear drumming and chanting on the far side. He had no idea who it was and he hadn't been invited to join the party, but he sure couldn't stay *here*. So he stepped back a few paces, lowered his brass helmeted head like a bull, and got set to charge.

On the far side, the Indians assembled in the ancient cave shrine had a totally different perspective. None of the pagan descendants of the priests who'd walled off the cave behind the altar could read the glyphs under the carved bas relief of Great Kukulcan. So they had no idea there was supposed to *be* anything on the far side of the wall. They weren't even looking at the wall. All eyes of the assembly were on the naked girl four male priests were holding down, face up, on the low stone slab in front of Xoc The Thirsty's black stone statue. Xoc held his bowl empty, waiting for human blood. The high priestess stood over the victim, gripping an obsidian sacrificial knife as she waited for the chanting God Singers to give her the signal. It was very important to do everything right in the cavern of gods. They needed rain. They needed help from Xoc, who stood only second to Kukulcan himself in power. But Xoc wouldn't help them with his life-giving rain unless the death they offered him was performed just right. As the old wise ones explained, when it didn't rain after they'd given blood to Xoc, it was because they'd done something wrong.

They were getting to the demand for blood. The priestess bit her lower lip and braced herself as she stared down at the frightened sacrifice. The two girls were almost the same age. The priestess, Humming Bird, felt sorry for the other girl. But they needed rain. She raised the knife, the torch lights gleaming on the green beetle-wing bracelets around her tawny naked arms. And then all hell broke loose.

The carved stonewall, after standing over a thousand years, exploded inward as the big American crashed through it, using his helmeted head as a battering ram. The priestess screamed and dropped her knife to cower away from the apparition of horror, as Captain Gringo staggered into the stone statue of Xoc and bumped heads

149

with it. The brass being tougher than brittle rock, Xoc lost his head and the helmet rang like a big brass gong. Captain Gringo roared with pain as he got his balance and stood there swaying, with ringing ears and eyes filled with stars. The men holding the sacrificial victim released her and ran for the nearest exit as the girl screamed mindlessly, convinced the god had come for her in the flesh!

Humming Bird wanted out, too, but she bumped into the wall and froze, wide-eyed with terror to shout, "No!" as one of the other priests, either crazy or made of sterner stuff, rushed at the monster who'd decapitated his favorite god and swung his club-sword with an overhand killing blow.

The weapon shattered on the brass helmet as the man trapped inside growled, "Oh, shit!" and fired his .38 through the rubberized canvas. A gout of flame shot forth from the heart of the monster and, as the attacker went down with a slug in his own chest, Humming Bird threw herself down at Captain Gringo's feet to wail, "Spare us, Mighty Kukulcan! We didn't know you had returned!"

The others started catching on, now that the priestess had pointed out the obvious. So there stood Captain Gringo with smoke drifting out of his chest and a cave full of Indians writhing around on the floor at his feet. Naturally, he didn't understand their Mayan words, but he got the idea they wanted to be friends. So he sat down on the sacrificial stone and decided he'd better get out of this Goddamn suit before he suffocated. His head had cleared enough for him to figure out how. Albeit not enough to consider the consequences. It was dumb, he now saw, to have forgotten the pen knife in his pants pocket all this time.

So as Humming Bird cautiously raised her head to see what the god had to say, she gagged in horror as she saw the little steel blade pop out of Kukulcan's chest. The uncanny being seemed to be skinning himself alive from inside!

As Captain Gringo heaved off the helmet and took a

deep breath, a Doubting Thomas in a back pew shouted, "Behold! It's not a god! It's a man! A white man! It was all a trick!"

Fortunately for him, since the bemused Captain Gringo still had his .38 out, Humming Bird rose on her knees to shout, imperiously, "Silence, you fool! Don't the old legends say Kukulcan was a white man when he chose to walk among humans from his home in the Eastern Sea! Look! He is shedding his god skin as a serpent sheds it's own! It *is* the mighty feather serpent! Who else could smash the image of Xoc and live? The legends tell us He promised to return if we ever really needed Him!"

There was a murmur of awed agreement as Captain Gringo finished climbing out of the ruined diving suit. He smiled at Humming Bird and asked, in Spanish, "Can you tell me the way to Don Fernando's hacienda, Doll Face?"

Humming Bird blushed at the god's compliment and replied in the same language, "You have come to lead the attack on the hated strangers, Oh Kukulcan? Good, we shall follow you to the death! But why are we speaking Spanish? Have you forgotten Maya?"

Catching on, he nodded and said, "Well, it's been a long time, Querida."

She stared adoringly at him, and that wasn't hard to take, since, aside from wearing little more than beetle wings and feathers she was a pretty little thing. She said, "Oh, I see you have spent the last thousand years over on the far side of the sea, among the white savages. May I ask why you were unable to show them the way, as you did for our ancestors?"

"I was travelling incognito. There are some rival gods over there I didn't want to meet until I got the goods on them. You can stand in my presence, Muchacha. What's your name?"

"My true name is Humming Bird. The Cristianos call me Dolores. Alas, one of my grandfathers was a white chiciero and they keep trying to turn me into a disbeliever. That is why I speak Spanish. They had me a prisoner in a mission school until I was old enough to run away to people of my true faith."

He nodded, sagely. He was willing to forgive her white grandfather, who must have been a damned nice-looking guy, from the way her partly European features turned out. The extra height she's inherited, as well as her better education, probably accounted for her being some kind of priestess. She was about five two, tall for a Maya, and built nicer than her sort of squatty tribespeople. He had to keep her on his side. So he decided he'd better not stare at her bare nipples. She seemed to be some kind of pagan nun. It sure seemed a waste. But that other little gal they'd been about to cut open would have been a waste, too. She was still cowering on the floor, beyond Humming Bird. He told the priestess, "All right. New rules. Pending further revelations, tell your people us gods don't want any more sacrifices."

Humming Bird frowned and asked, "No sacrifices? How are you and the other gods to live without food?"

He shook his head and said, "You people just haven't been thinking. I meant to explain it the last time I dropped by, but, as you know, I had to leave in a hurry. The gods create everything here on Earth, no?"

"Of course, Great Kukulcan! Even the very air we breathe is sent to us by the gods. That's why we must give you presents, no?"

"Poor logic, Humming Bird. When a man builds a house, does he expect the house to tear out some of it's own bricks and give them back to him? One of the reasons I came back here this evening was to tell you we're getting damned annoyed about this sacrifice nonsense. Its not easy to make a pretty girl like that one over there, you know, and you were about to ruin all our work. Humans can't give presents to gods, Humming Bird. If a god wants something, he or she just whips it up for themselves, see?"

Humming Bird nodded, cautiously, and said, "I never looked at things that way before. I praise you for the revelation!" Then she pointed at the busted statue to add, "But if Xoc did not wish for blood, tonight, as he has on many other nights, why didn't *he* tell us?"

"That's why I knocked his block off. Old Xoc always has been a surly cuss. Tell your people it's all over for tonight. I'll let you know when I have further orders for them."

Humming Bird turned and translated the commands of Kukulcan to the others. Most were too awed to argue. But there's always some trouble-maker in any group. So an old goat with his face painted black stepped forward to argue theology. As he stood there shaking a feather duster at Captain Gringo and shouting, Humming Bird explained, "He is a priest of Xoc and he says you are only a human being."

Captain Gringo nodded soberly, raised the gun, and blew the old man's black face to jam. It seemed sort of brutal, but what the hell, the priests of Xoc seemed to like blood.

That settled the matter, as far as the others were concerned. After being off somewhere, all those years, Kukulcan seemed to have returned in a vile mood. So he soon found himself alone with the priestess and the girl she'd been about to carve up when he burst in on them.

He smiled and said, "My, isn't this cozy? I have to be on my way, girls. But first let me ask you a few questions."

"We are your slaves, Oh Kukulcan!" Humming Bird said.

He told his groin to simmer down. She probably meant that in a religious sense. Even if she didn't, he had to haul ass before the superstitious Maya wised up. He said, "I've come back on a mission for the other gods. As you see, I'm trying to pass as a mortal. Do you think I look human enough to fool the white people?"

She said. "Well, you are too big and beautiful to be a real human, but the Cristianos are very stupid."

"Good. We know all about Don Fernando and his

chicleros. Some of my fellow gods are waiting for me at his hacienda now, pretending to be human. Have your people been having trouble with Don Fernando?"

"Not really what you could call trouble, Adored Master. The chicleros do not molest us, since the trees they seek do not grow in our corn milpas and we chew very little gum once we grow up. But of course they are Cristianos who follow the wrong faith, no?"

Captain Gringo nodded soberly as he answered, "I know for a fact that Don Fernando and his wife follow secret fertility rites their church doesn't approve of, so let's give them a break. I want you to tell your people to leave the local chicleros alone."

"I will do as you wish, Oh Kukulcan, but what about the *other* white men, the mad and wicked ones?"

He nodded again, wondering how she kept that little feather apron in place between her brown thighs, as he said, "Tell me about them."

She said, with a puzzled frown he didn't like at all, "Do you not know about them, Master? I thought the gods knew everything."

"Oh, we do," he hastily reassured her, adding, "That's one of the main reasons I came back. I know evil men have come into your country, cutting down trees and stirring up trouble. I wanted to hear what you and your people have to say about them, see?"

She nodded, with restored faith, and said, "It is as you saw from your home out in the sea, Oh Kukulcan. The strangers are not Spanish speakers. They are all crazy, and some of them are *bad*! The ones who cut down the mahogany trees and then shove them into cenotes are probably just crazy. But the ones who stand around with guns, just watching, are evil as well. When some of our people approached to ask them why they stuffed trees in wells, the strangers shot them down like dogs without answering. My people are very angry. Even the Hispanic priests who used to burn our batabobs at the stake usually at least *said* something, first!"

"Yes, I can see how that would annoy anyone," he murmured, trying to think of his next best move. He'd confirmed what he'd suspected about the mahogany pirates smuggling the purloined lumber across the border, even if he had lost Sir Cedric's diving suit in the process. He asked, "Can you tell me which way the cenotes drain, Humming Bird?"

She frowned and said, "To the south, of course! Didn't you know that? You just *came up* from the underworld, Master!"

"Just testing you. We gods don't like to have ignorant priestesses."

It worked. She smiled, lowering her lashes, pleased at the compliment. So, okay, he was in good shape for the moment, alone in this cave with two dead men, too nearly naked ladies and a busted statue. But it was probably not a good idea to ask for directions back to the hacienda. Gods were not supposed to get lost. He had his compass and there was a full moon either rising or risen, depending on what time it was. He took out his watch, nodded, and said, "I'll be leaving as soon as the moon comes up. Are we straight on your orders, Humming Bird? No more human sacrifices and no more raiding the surrounding settlers?"

She nodded and said, "Orders from the gods must be obeyed. But what about the bad men who shoot at us, deeper in jungle? Are we allowed to fight with *them*?"

It was tempting. But he'd proven to his own satisfaction that spears and sword-clubs weren't such a hot idea against guns, and the mahogany pirates obviously were guarded by hired guns. He said. "Tell your people not to worry about them anymore. The other gods and me will take care of them our own way."

Humming Bird glanced at the smashed idol and the two bodies across the cave and smiled like a she-tiger as she purred, "Oh, I almost feel sorry for them, wicked as they are!"

The naked girl who's sacrifice he'd broken up didn't

have any clue as to what they were talking about, of course, but as she'd watched and seen the god who'd saved her wasn't to shoot any more lightning bolts from his heart, she plucked up her courage to ask Humming Bird something in their own musical tongue.

The pretty priestess nodded and said, "Singing Fish wishes to know if you want her, now, Oh, Kukulcan."

He frowned and said, "I just said no more cutting people open with stone knives, damn it."

"I know. She did not mean it that way. She wants to know if you wish to take her virginity. We chose her tonight for Xoc because she was a virgin, of course. But you have won her from Xoc, so she says she is yours, to do with as you wish."

Captain Gringo stared soberly at the frightened teenager, knowing exactly what he'd like to do to her indeed. But he said, "Tell her these are my orders. I accept her as one of my chosen people. But she's to go home and grow up. I want her to get married, have lots of kids, and live happily ever after in my honor."

Humming Bird translated. Singing Fish looked at him adoringly, came over to him, and fell at his feet, sobbing in gratitude. He said, "Aw, mush. Send her home, Humming Bird."

So the priestess did, and as they regarded one another alone in the flickering torch light, he saw he was almost in the clear, if he could find a graceful way to get rid of her.

He couldn't go back the way he'd come, without the diving suit. He'd wait a while, douse the lights, and slip away, once it got really dark. He knew the red sky at this time, outside, would reveal him to any other doubting Thomases in this neck of the woods. If he could put some distance between himself and here before moonrise, he had to head west by compass until he hit the open savannah. From there it would be easy.

Humming Bird said, "I know why you sent her away. She was one of the common people, no?"

He nodded absently and said, "Something like that." So Humming Bird walked to the sacrificial stone, took off her little feather apron, and lay across the altar with her thighs spread invitingly. He noticed she had no hair between her legs as she sighed, "I am so honored it was me you chose, Mighty Kukulcan!"

He gulped. There was a time and place for everything. The place she was offering for inspection was very tempting, too. But he had to get out of here before they wised up! Humming Bird lay with her eyes closed, already hot with anticipation. He didn't want her doubting him. Since Hell hath no fury like a woman scorned, he was in danger of turning her into a pissed off athiest!

So he went over to the wall, pulled out one torch after another, and started dousing them. As they were plunged into darkness, he heard her sigh, "Oh, you are so merciful. You were afraid the sight of you in full glory would blind me with it's radiance, no!"

He muttered, "close enough," as he groped his way to her, opened his shirt and dropped his pants, but hung on to the gun as he put out the other hand to find her. He wound up with the hand on her firm little breast. So everything else just sort of fell in place as he got to his knees in front of the low slab and mounted her. As his engorged erection entered her, Humming Bird gasped with delight, "Oh, my God!"

He said, "Hell, at times like this it's all right for you to just call me Kukulcan."

As he started moving in her hairless passionate opening, Humming Bird sobbed, "Oh, if ever there was any doubt you were a god, I know *now,* you *are!* Is it permissable to have an orgasm, Lord and Master? I am trying to be reverent, but . . . "

"Oh, go ahead, I'm an easy going god."

"Ooooh, I'd hardly call that easy and I'm . . . comingggggg!"

So he did, too. And then he knew he had to have more of this lovely little savage, so he braced his hands on the slab in a push-up position, gun to one side and legs out straight, to really give it to her with one of her knees hooked over either of his locked elbows. She was moving like she thought she was in heaven, which she probably did. There was a lot to be said for this god business. A woman honored by a god's long donging just kept having repeated orgasms instead of asking him if he was married or if he'd still respect her in the morning. By the time he'd had her three times, Humming Bird had lost count of her own orgasms and between her superstition and what was, after all, a pretty good screwing by a skilled and well-hung lover, she passed out.

When she regained consciousness, Humming Bird sat up, still throbbing warmly between her legs, and called out, "Kukulcan, Dear?"

There was no answer. Humming Bird knew she was alone in the cave shrine. She gasped, "Oh, he vanished back into the spirit world, just the way he came! Isn't it amazing? He certainly felt like a real man inside me!"

She groped in the darkness for her apron and put it back on, along with her headress that had somehow fallen off while the god was honoring her. She staggered outside, legs wobbly and groin still tingling. But as she saw the others waiting with torches and expressions of awe, the priestess drew herself up imperiously and said, "The God has left again. But I have a message for you all."

One of the Mayan men looked puzzled and asked, "Which way did he go? We just got here, having heard someone desecrated the shrine of Xoc."

"Idiot!" snapped Humming Bird. "There was no desecration. Xoc is dead. Kukulcan killed him. We shall seal up the cave and forget Xoc. I am the chosen mortal lover of the Feathered Serpent! So from now on I shall lead you in my lord and master's way!"

Don Fernando and his wife probably slept together at night, for the novelty, because Miguelito was pulling night watch when Captain Gringo got to the hacienda shortly after midnight, after doing some artful dodging and getting turned around a few times. As he walked into the moonlit compound a chained dog barked and Miguelito swaggered out in his *muy macho charro* outfit to demand, *"Quien es?"*

And then he saw Captain Gringo in the moonlight and fainted on the spot. Captain Gringo chuckled, stepped over him, and kept going. He didn't get to the main house. He went to the servant quarters where Gaston and Black Lolita were shacked up. He saw a light under Gaston's door and opened it without knocking. Apparently Lolita was bisexual as well as black, since she was going sixty-nine with little Ynez while Gaston went in and out of the statuesque Juanita in the more customary position, at the other end of the bed. All three girls screamed when they saw Captain Gringo and even Gaston lost his usual composure as he gasped, "Dick! We thought you were dead!"

Captain Gringo said, "I noticed. Okay, now that you've all consoled one another, get dressed. We're moving out. Tell the others not to blab too much about it. I hate good-byes in the first place and don't want to tell anyone here at the hacienda where we're headed in the second."

Later, however, as they left the hacienda and he counted noses in the moonlight, he saw they were short a few heads. The distance between the hacienda and Puerto Barrios and the Guatemalan Law had prompted some of the men to sign on with Don Fernando for the free and easy life of the chiclero. The chicleros already here being short of women, all but Lolita, Juanita and Ynez had decided they were tired of being adelitas, too. So aside from Gaston he was down to four loyal men and three oversexed girls.

It was probably just as well. Even Gaston objected when Captain Gringo told him what came next. He said, "Dick, our orders were to stay inside the borders of Guatamala, non?"

"Yeah," Captain Gringo replied, "and we agreed to stop the mahogany pirates, too. San Lorenzo's at the head of navigation on the Rio Belize. We'll beg, borrow or steal a balsa there and shoot the rapids downstream until we find the bankside cave they're using to squirt logs out into the main river. It'll probably be in a stretch of quiet water."

"*Oui,* but inside British Honduras, where our hunting permit from Guatamala is no good!"

"Relax. We're not likely to tangle with any British constabulary. The other guys are crooks. So they'll be set up somewhere the British Colonial government isn't policing, see?"

"You mean, assuming said authorities are not on it with them, don't you, Dick? How do you know the Royal Governor isn't getting a cut? Money talks and that mahogany is worth a fortune, no?"

"Mahogany is worth a lot of money yes. But the crooks don't have police protection."

"Ah, they told you this themselves? When did they take you into their confidence, Sage Leader?"

Captain Gringo smiled thinly and replied, "When the *Imperial Trader* ran us down and left us to the sharks, of course. That was pretty shifty, even for a puffed up

160

Lime Juicer. Anyone who's steamed the seas long enough to make Master would have stopped for us unless he'd had a reason not to. The skipper of the *Imperial Trader* had a reason. He didn't want strangers to board his vessel, even soaking wet."

Gaston nodded and said, "Ah, *oui*, had he brought us into Belize there would gave been an inquiry about the collision at sea, too. Very well, we can assume he and his friends are wary about the British lawmen in Belize. What do you imagine he had aboard that we were not supposed to see, though? I can't see them smuggling mahogany *in* to Belize!"

"Of course not. He may have had a deck cargo of guns. That's the most profitable cargo ships coming in from Europe carry. Naturally, he'd have unloaded them somewhere along the coast before steaming into Belize so innocently."

"And, of course, he would not wish anyone but his crew to see him do so. It works. But we were not off British Honduras when that steamer ran us down, Dick. We were off the Nicaraguan coast. I thought the revolution in Nicaragua was over for the season, non?"

"It was when the guys we were helping down there lost. I'm still working on that angle. If there's a library in San Lorenzo I'd better catch up on my reading. I haven't been paying much attention to things this far north."

"Neither have I. Perhaps someone is planning a revolution in British Honduras?"

"Nobody but the brits themselves have the money to plan much of anything in a British Colony. They learned that from us Yanks and the Irish. A revolution needs leaders. There were hardly any Hispanics living in British Honduras when the Crown decided it would look nice on the map in 'Imperial Pink.' So almost everyone there who can read and write is British. They imported English speaking blacks from their West Indian possessions to cut the cane and sweep the floors. They're well-paid and well-treated for common labor in this part of the world and, if they revolt, they have no way to get home to Jamaica or Trinidad. I'd say Queen Vickie is safe from any revolutions in these parts for at least a couple of generations. Besides, if the smugglers were working with anyone out to overthrow the colonial government they'd be pretty stupid, since it would mess up their profitable mahogany operation."

"*Oui,* if they are running guns as a side line, it must be to the rebels in Nicaragua or even Guatemala. Did you hear anything about a budding revolt in Puerto Barrios while we were there, Dick?"

Captain Gringo shook his head, frowned and answered, "That sexy police informant gave me some guff about being against the Guatemalan government while we were playing slap and tickle. Naturally she was trying to draw me out so she could report what I said to the cops. But if they weren't worried about a rebel party they wouldn't be asking questions like that. Yeah, it works. Major Llamas sent a half-ass guerrilla to check out rumors of a distant threat because his army's keeping a lid on something closer to home!"

"Let us pick up the pace, then," Gaston said looking up at the moon. "If we don't finish and get back to Puerto Barrios before the revolution starts, we may have a time getting *paid,* hein?"

San Lorenzo was a little mission village. It had no public library, but a friendly priest allowed Captain Gringo the use of his rectory library while he arranged a balsa for them. The priest was called Padre Alejandro and he approved of Captain Gringo's taming the pagan Maya for the moment, since Captain Gringo left out the fun parts.

The magazines and newspapers were hopelessly out of date, but Padre Alejandro must have liked to read. He had bound volumes of everything from the *Almanac de Gotha* to *The Prisoner of Zenda* on his shelves. Captain Gringo selected a few items of interest to brouse through as he killed some time. *The World Atlas* was printed in Spain and didn't even have the Rio Belize on its small-scale map of Central America. So they could worry about the rapids when they came to them.

Padre Alejandro came back to say, "I managed to get you a large balsa, my son. At the moment your French compadre and the others are loading your supplies aboard it. But surely you will not be leaving us now? The morning grows late. La Siesta will find you out on the open water in the sun, no?"

Captain Gringo returned the book he'd been reading to the shelf as he said, "I hope so, Padre. How far are we from the border?"

"About thirty or forty kilometers, allowing for bends in the river. That is the point I am trying to make, my son. Where will you and the others shelter during the siesta hours?"

"On the raft, of course. It'll be cooler on the water."

He didn't tell the priest the real reason. Padre Alejandro might not understand his views of the law. He followed the priest from the mission and sure enough, the balsa Gaston had just finished loading was a stout-looking river-runner, about thirty feet long, with it's logs well-lashed and sweeps mounted fore and aft. Gaston had put most of the supplies and the machinegun amid ships. The Maxim was under a tarp, but mounted atop the supplies so its muzzle could sweep in all directions. The mules, of course, not only had to stay here in San Lorenzo, but had more than paid for the balsa.

They were missing another guy, too. One of the men who'd signed on to escape jail in Puerto Barrios had decided he liked it here in San Lorenzo. Gaston agreed that looking for him would be pointless. So, as Padre Alejandro waved farewell up on the red clay bank, they shoved off.

The river looked placid enough as it ran past the mission town, but the current was moving pretty good. Captain Gringo looked his three last soldados over and asked if any of them knew beans about running rapids. A heavy set guy as black as Lolita said he was called Cascadero and that he'd been a river-runner before a false-hearted woman got him in trouble with the law. Captain Gringo didn't ask Cascadero if he'd stolen for her or murdered her. He put him on the forward sweep. He wanted Gaston steering with the after sweep, since he could count on the Frenchman there in a running gunfight along the riverbank. That left the other two guys and the three girls with nothing much to do. So he told them to sit around the supplies amid ships and behave themselves. The burly Cascadero got the square bow, if you wanted to call it that, aimed down the way they were being carried by the current. Captain Gringo stood by Gaston at the other end and checked the chambers of his .38 as he asked Gaston, "What do you know about the other folks still with us, Gaston?"

Gaston said, "Well, Juanita has the best body, Ynez has the tightest cunt, and Lolita sucks with enthusiasm."

"Goddamn it, I know about the *women*! How come these last two guys didn't desert with the others?"

"Oh, they're a team. They commit highway robbery and sodomy together every chance they get. Pancho, the big one, is the husband. Naturally, little Joselito is the girl. They either came along because they are loyal or because, more probably, they don't make friends easily, and signed on to duck a death sentence they must have well deserved. Hispanics take both their vices *très* serious."

They came to a stretch of modestly white water. The girls and Joselito screamed as the balsa passed over the bump in the river. But Cascadero was as good at his sweep as Gaston was back here, so the balsa didn't broach at all. Captain Gringo hunkered down and lit a cigar as he studied his options. Three straight men and three nymphos worked out about right. The two mariposas were probably tough or they wouldn't be tagging along. Cascadero was shaping up nicely and the three experienced adelitas could handle guns in a pinch. So, okay, allowing that half the people on any side tended to shirk in a fire fight, he had eight guns, one of them a machinegun, which would make up for some shirking indeed. Those were not great odds, if the guys he was hunting came in serious numbers. But he had surprise as well as the Maxim in his corner. He'd come out on top in stickier situations.

Juanita got up and came aft, demanding, "When are we to stop for La Siesta, muchachos? It is already getting hot."

Captain Gringo peered up at her and growled, "Watch that muchacho shit. My rank is still capitano, whether I've fraternized with the troops or not."

Juanita laughed, hands on hips, and said, "That is what

165

I had in mind, Deek. I will call you a *general,* if you like, but the other girls and me wish to find some shade where we can get out of this stupid sun and into some more fucking."

Captain Gringo laughed, "Save it for now, Querida. I want to cross the border during the siesta hour. By the way, one of you three ought to start making eyes at Cascadero. This orgy stuff is fun, but we have to keep up our strength. We seem to have four natural couples aboard this balsa. So we'd better sort it out."

Juanita frowned and asked, "Four? We girls are only three and . . . . Oh, I see what you mean. Which of us do *you* choose, Deek?"

"Hell, you're all lovely. I'll let you girls decide."

"That won't work, Querido. You are the best-looking man aboard."

Gaston sighed, "Thank's a lot. She's right, Dick. You'll have to choose everyone's partner for tonight, assuming we are still alive tonight, hein?"

Captain Gringo puffed his cigar as he thought about that. Juanita was built, but Ynez was prettier. On the other hand, he'd had them both and, since this was simple lust and not romance, why not go for novelty?

He said, "All right, I'll sleep with Lolita tonight."

Gaston quickly added, "I'll take Ynez, flat chested or not. I prefer a snug fit, if one must go steady."

"Damn," Juanita said, "that leaves me to the Negro."

Captain Gringo said, "Try to be liberal. I think you're prettier than the black girl, too. But it could be taken the wrong way if we put the two blacks in the party together and, face it, Juanita, you know you like novelty, too."

She laughed, lewdly, and said, "Well, Cascadero is big. I will decide how big, later."

As she moved forward to inform the others of the new developments Gaston chuckled and said, "Wise move, Dick. I forgot to tell you Lolita is mad about white meat. That is why she'll even go down in bed with a woman of lighter complexion."

166

"Knock it off. You're letting us drift to one side. I'm not worried about fucking. I'm worried about fighting, if the border guards aren't taking their siesta when we float past."

Gaston nodded and said, "I thought that was why we were frying our brains out here on the river. Didn't they send us up here to fight people from Honduras, my truculent youth?"

"Yeah, that's why I don't want to have to fight the Guatemalan border guards if we can avoid it. We'll have one hell of a time getting paid by Guatemala if we do."

"Agreed. It's not too late to pull over to the bank and ravage the maidens in the shrubbery, you know."

"Keep up in mid-current, damn it. You're talking like an idiot, even for you."

"Merde alors," Gaston protested, "you say *I* am speaking foolishly? It's not my idea to invade another country against orders, Dick!"

"Fuck the orders! You wanted to head for Belize to begin with. We agreed to fight the mahogany pirates and they're not in Guatemala. Not the big shots, anyhow. I don't see any sense in shooting simple loggers. The gang would just get new ones. The only way to end this bullshit is to cut off their pipeline."

Up ahead, Cascadero shouted a warning and the next few minutes were sort of frantic as the balsa went through white water indeed. No boat could have made it, even with the burly black and the skillful Gaston working as a team. But the big spongy logs could take the rocks they hit going through lickety-split for what felt like a million miles.

Then, at last, they were drifting on calm water again, moving faster now. Everyone was drenched, of course. Lolita came aft, her white cotton clinging to her curvaceous black body as, avoiding Gaston's eye, she asked Captain Gringo what she and the other girls should do about their wet clothes. He said, "Don't take them off. People along the bank are already likely to be curious about us, Lolita. Besides, it's cooler out here under the sun with our clothes wet."

She said, "I am afraid of getting a sun tan. I do not wish to get any darker."

He didn't see how that would be possible, for, despite her rather Spanish features, Lolita was already ebony black and, now that he could see through her dress, built better than he'd recalled from the one time he'd seen her naked—on the bottom. "You won't get sun burned," he said. "We seem to be passing through more trees, now. We'll soon be in the jungle."

She nodded and volunteered, "I hope so. I have to watch my complexion lest people take me for a Negress. Is it . . . true you said you wished for me to be your adelita, Deek?"

"Later. We have to get across the border before we can even think about the future, Querida."

Crossing into British Honduras was anticlimatic. As Captain Gringo had hoped, nobody was standing watch along the riverbank as they whipped through Bengue Viejo at a good clip amid stream. Who would they have been expecting? It was a well-established fact in these parts that nobody with a brain in his head would be travelling during the heat of day in the dry season.

The British outpost a few miles further downstream at Cayo seemed to be manned by sensible guards, too. So they were in the clear. The map said there wasn't another town for miles.

The map left out the next stretch of rapids, and it was a pisser. They hit a rock and broached broadside to the raging white water despite all Gaston and Cascadero could do. Fortunately, just as all seemed lost, the balsa hit an even bigger rock that knocked Pancho overboard and straightened them out. As they drifted into quiet water again Joselito was running up and down the side of the raft, screaming, "Pancho, Querido, where are you?"

Captain Gringo shielded his eyes against the sun as he stared out across the water, too. He spotted Pancho's head a couple of hundred yards downstream and called out, "Cascadero! Swing starboard and we'll pick him up!"

They would have, too, if the bobbing head hadn't suddenly vanished with an anguished scream. Joselito screamed, too, yelling, "Oh, my God a cayman has him!"

Captain Gringo stared morosely at the red foam rising from the water where Pancho had been taken by the big reptile and muttered, "When you're right you're right. Remind us never to go swimming in the Rio Belize! I didn't know the crocodile tribe liked fast moving water."

Gaston said, "I think it's the animals swept away by the current they really like. In Africa, the biggest crocodiles on earth are to be found below the falls of the Congo. But I digress. Regard the banks on either side, Dick."

Captain Gringo nodded as he stared at the low, but white vertical walls the swift current had cut through the limestone on its way to the sea. He said, "Yeah. They'll have to get higher, though. There has to be a high enough bank for a cave to form in above water level. Those logs would hang up on the ceiling if it was all under water under the surface. I'd better go comfort Joselito."

He walked forward toward the still prancing and distraught catamite, saying, "I'm sorry, Joselito. I can see he meant a lot to you."

Joselito stopped, turned, and stared owlishly for a moment before he blurted, "It's your fault my Pancho is dead! You killed him, you Yanqui brute!"

Naturally, Captain Gringo went for his own gun at the same time. But before he could draw, Lolita grabbed Joselito from behind and threw him overboard. He hit with a mighty splash, came up screaming, then went under again and stayed there. Captain Gringo didn't know if another cayman had taken him, or if Joselito just hadn't known how to swim. He turned to Lolita and said, "Thank you. I didn't know you were so strong."

The pretty black girl shrugged and said, "I am your adelita. Adelitas are supposed to be strong, no?"

He smiled at her. He was sure glad he hadn't chosen Ynez. Ynez wasn't big enough to have done the deed. She and Juanita had been sitting there with Lolita when

Joselito went nuts. They were probably annoyed at him for some reason.

He started to move aft to rejoin Gaston, reshuffling the odds, now that he'd just lost two more men. The odds were getting lousy. What chance did three men and three women have against a gang that could number any number you wanted to worry about?

He got to find out. As he was passing the supplies, Cascadero shouted. Captain Gringo turned as the current carried them around a bend between two higher banks on either side. The river had swirled around in here a few million years to cut through the limestone rise. He recognized it as the same ridge running inside the Guatemalan border further north.

The current slowed as the river widened in the natural amphitheater. A steam launch was tied up near the maw of the big cave in the high bank. Men in canoes were paddling around to pole floating logs together. They looked startled to see the raft come round the bend. They had every right to be. Even as Captain Gringo was tearing the cover off the machinegun, another huge mahogany log popped out of the cave mouth like a swimming cayman and, over on the launch, some son-of-a-bitch was shooting at them with a rifle! Like all pirates, the mahogany pirates knew dead men told no tales, so they hadn't waited to ask questions!

Captain Gringo yelled, "Everybody behind these boxes!" as he fed a round into the Maxim's chamber with only his head and shoulders exposed behind the weapon. A rifle round smashed into a supply box near his elbow. So he started firing back as Gaston crouched at his side, feeding the belt while keeping his head down. Captain Gringo didn't look to see if the girls and Cascadero were there. He was too busy peering down the sights at the steam launch. The Maxim cleared its throat with a roar of hot lead, churning up a line of white spray as Captain Gringo traversed left and hosed the launch with bullets along the waterline before he elevated and scythed back the other way at rail level. The launch's boiler exploded in a huge cloud of scalding steam and, when it cleared, the launch wasn't there any more.

Captain Gringo ignored the scalded crew men screaming in the water as a moron in one of the smaller canoes ticked his hat brim with a rifle round. He snarled, "I was saving you for *dessert*!" as he tap danced machinegun bullets the length of the dugout, spilling its contents in the cayman infested water. They screamed a lot, too, as the ever ravenous caymans took them one by one. But Captain Gringo was too busy smoking up the other canoes, and their crews, to notice the swirls of scaley tails as the big hungry reptiles pulled their victims under!

Then, after a while, there was nobody to shoot at, so he stopped shooting, as the current carried them downstream. He stared at a straw hat floating along side in the current and muttered, "Nuts. We can't go ashore to mop up."

Gaston got to his feet, saying "*Merde alors,* what could there be to *mop*? Anyone still alive is stranded for the moment. It should take them some time to be back in operation. By then we will have been paid for this good day's work and be on our way back to Costa Rica, hein?"

Captain Gringo nodded and said, "Guess so. We'll see when we reach Belize."

"We are still going to Belize? When did this mad thought occur to you, Dick?"

"The first time we hit serious white water, of course. How the hell would you suggest we get this raft back up the river?"

Gaston nodded but said, "That is of course not possible, I agree. But we still have our legs. Those English people we met at Don Fernando's said they marched in from the coast, non?"

"Yeah, with porters and a guide, on a mapped path. I had all the jungle running by guesswork I cared for last night, Gaston. This country is a real bitch. If you won't stumble into a cenote you keep running into tangles you wouldn't believe. The Indians are slash and burn farmers. So there's a lot of abandoned milpas gone to crazy seed. I don't *like* hacking through man-sized artichokes or saw grass over my head. We'll be safer doing things the easy way. Nobody in the British colonial government should get excited about white men coming *out* of the jungle they own."

"Perhaps. But what do we say should they see fit to ask?"

"Shit, I'll tell them I'm Sir Cedric and that you're my wife. Don't fret about it, Gaston. We have to follow this current to Belize whether we want to or not. Besides, the *Imperial Trader* will be moored there and we still owe them. The shits we just killed were minor members of the team."

Rafting down the river to Belize was easy enough, now that they'd gotten past the worst rapids and settled the hash of the punks they'd been sent to stop. But the current slowed as they got into the lowlands. So nightfall found them still on the Rio Belize. They pulled into a sandbar out in mid-stream. Camping here for the night would keep them safe from the mosquitos and other jungle critters that might bite them to death in their sleep. Captain Gringo told the others not to build a fire. They were only a few miles from the coastal settlements now, and while there was a little brushy cover growing on the island, he didn't want to explain what they were doing there to a British river patrol if someone spotted a fire. So they ate their frijoles cold and then, since it had been a hard day, with a harder one probably facing them, he told everybody to bed down.

He unrolled his own bedding near the set-up machine-gun, on the down-stream end of the bar. He'd forgotten about Lolita until the black adelita shyly joined him. Then he noticed in the moonlight that she'd taken all her clothes off and wondered how it had been possible to forget anything like that.

Lolita was quiet until they got in the roll together. Then he saw he wasn't going to get much sleep. He'd noticed when she threw Joselito over the side that she looked

174

strong. She hauled his last boot off and threw herself full length on his back as she purred, "I wish to be vile with you!" Then, as she crouched over him with her muscular ebony knees between his naked legs and bent to inhale his bemused and still limp shaft, he said, "Be my guest!" and lay back, staring up at the tropic stars, to enjoy it.

He hadn't chosen her because he wanted to lay her in particular. She was pretty, he wasn't picky about what shade a pretty girl came wrapped in, and he'd shared women with Gaston before. But she was coming with the possessive bit and he didn't know what he'd do with her once they got to Belize.

The Brits could get silly about a white man with a black companion of either sex. On the other hand, he didn't want anyone to invite him to tea at the yacht club in Belize. He needed a shave, and his clothes were quickly getting trail-worn. If they took him for a beachcomber who'd "sunk" to the level of the local blacks, they might not want to talk to him, and that was jake with him. He didn't want to talk to anyone in authority, either.

Lolita looked up from what she was doing and purred, "Oh, one sees there is more to you than I expected. You are *muy grande,* for a blanco!"

She had him *muy grande* indeed, so he pulled her up beside him, lay her on her back, and mounted her to do it right. She spread her long, black, shapely legs in astounding welcome, like she meant to take him balls and all. But as he entered her, he discovered to his pleasure that she was built as tightly as the much smaller Ynez, while as shapely as Juanita. As he started moving in her, Lolita gasped, "Oh, be careful, my toro! I have never taken a man as big as you, in every way."

"No shit? I thought you meant I was big for a white man. Is that *true,* by the way? I've never been screwed by a black guy, so I've had to take it as an article of faith that they're hung better."

She grimaced and started moving her hip in time with his thrusts as she said, "I would not know. I never give

175

myself to Los Negros. I am too proud. I have blanco blood on both sides, so I do not consider myself black."

He didn't answer—he was too busy, but after he'd climaxed and slowed down to a steady canter in the saddle, he was glad he hadn't tried to palm her off on Cascadero. As he'd suspected, she was trying to prove she was sort of white by getting next to all the white meat she could.

After she'd come the first time and relaxed a bit, she wrapped her legs around him, hugged him closer, and began to try and swallow his whole head alive. Her mouth wasn't big enough, but that didn't keep her from kissing him from ear to ear with her mouth wide open and her tongue exploring his features. It felt wild as hell when she took his whole ear in her thick but pretty lips and tried to shove her pink tongue through his ear drum. After he'd exploded in her like fashion, he let her get on top so he could kiss her dangling nipples as she moved up and down on his shaft. She must have liked it, for after he shot up into her she clamped down hard to milk it further as she collapsed weakly on him, sobbing, "Oh, I have not had such a lover in a long time! Do you mind if we just fuck, tonight, Querido? I know you men like the other business with the mouth and popo, but I do not wish for to waste any of this on anything but the real thing!"

He'd been hoping she wouldn't want to go sixty-nine. Neither of them had had a bath for a long time. And while the codfish reek of her sweating body made for good-old-hot-and-dirty screwing, enough was enough. So he moved inside her teasingly and said, "This is good enough for me."

She started moving again, too, as she sighed, "Oh, I am so glad you are a good sport, too."

In the morning, after risking a pot of hot coffee and cautious whore baths along the edge of the sandbar, they were on their way again. Gaston looked pleased with himself. Juanita must have enjoyed her night with Cascadero, from the look of tired satisfaction on her ugly face.

As Captain Gringo had suspected, they were only a couple of hours upstream from Belize. Nobody seemed interested as they drifted out into the estuary north of the little colonial town. Captain Gringo spotted the Union Jack drooping from a pole over some serious-looking walls ahead. So he told the others to start poling into the bank. They ran the balsa up on a muddy shore near an inland garbage dump. The only person who saw them was a little black boy grazing his small herd of goats by the dump. He waved. Captain Gringo waved back. As the boy drifted over, the tall American put the canvas wrapped machinegun ashore and asked, "Is there somewhere around here our stuff will be safe, muchacho?"

The boy frowned and answered, "What you say, mon?" and Captain Gringo realized he'd forgotten where he was and spoke Spanish. So he repeated the question in English and this time the kid grinned and said, "Mammy Crawford got a shanty near, mon. She hide you stuff, do you gives her money."

"If I give *you* some money, will you lead us there?"

The boy laughed and said, "Mon, you gives me money an' you kin fuck my sister! Make it twenty bob and I bends over myself!"

Captain Gringo took out some coins, knowing silver was legal tender even if it wasn't British coin of the realm. He said, "Here. I think this should be about worth a shilling, right?"

"Mon, it worth almost half a crown. How come you so rich? You folkses must be outlaws, right?"

Captain Gringo reminded himself not to be so generous in the future as he recalled what waiters he'd spoken to in the past said about the tipping habits of English travellers. He said, "We're not outlaws. I'm a prince travelling incognito with my court. How far is this shanty I just paid for?"

The boy pocketed the coin and pointed inland, saying, "Follow the path, mon. I got to stay here with my goats. Mammy Crawford's the only shanty you finds that way. She live alone 'cause she old and ugly and they say she a conjure woman."

Apparently Mammy Crawford thought she was a witch, too. When they got to her shanty in a grove of sea grape, she met them at the door jingling bells attached to a dried out chicken foot as she asked, "You want to know you' future, white boy?"

Captain Gringo crossed her palm with silver before he said, " I know my future looks lousy, Mammy. I want to leave some things and the people with me here while I run into town to see some friends. Do we have a deal?"

Mammy Crawford looked down at the coins in her palm and sighed, "Oh, don't we ever, though? You run along and I'll see to you' chillens, you sweet thing!"

So he told Cascadero to lug the gear up from the balsa and told the girls to behave themselves until he and Gaston got back. As the two white men walked away, Gaston said, "Well, that was neatly done, Dick. Now we only have ourselves to worry about, hein?"

Captain Gringo said, "It's tempting, but sort of shitty. None of them speak English and they're expecting us to get them back to Puerto Barrios and pay them off besides."

Gaston walked moodily beside him, puffing a bit as they went up a steep ridge. Then they stopped on the crest to see the town and harbor roads spread out to the east. Gaston said, "Eh bien, what now? Do you suppose we can book passage by simply walking in and asking directions to the ticket office, Dick?"

Captain Gringo pointed out across with his chin, saying, "We're in luck. There's the goddamn *Imperial Trader,* moored out in deep water! See those yachts along the quay down there? One of them should be the Neville's. We'll ask casually along the waterfront."

As they started down into town, Gaston asked, "What good will it do to find the yacht those English people came here aboard, Dick? They are still back at Don Fernando's, non?"

"I sure hope so. We're going to need that yacht to get out to the *Imperial Trader* tonight."

Gaston stopped in mid-stride, protesting, "Now I *know* you have gone insane! They'll never give us passage aboard that steamer, Dick!"

"Hey, who said anything about booking passage? We're going to sink the son-of-a-bitch!"

"Oh, that sounds more reasonable," Gaston said. "Not very reasonable, but at least possible, given the machine-gun, surprise, and a yacht. But speaking of shitty, my cutthroat of the high seas, I thought you *liked* Pam and Cedric Neville, non?"

Captain Gringo said, "Oh, Pam's all right, once you see her legs. But Cedric tried to kill me, so I'm a little annoyed at him."

"Really? I thought *you* cut that life-line, Dick."

"I did. I had to, when the son-of-a-bitch air-hose popped off that diving helmet like a poorly secured baby bottle nipple. He was the prick who put me in that diving suit, and he was supposed to be an experienced diver, so forget accidents. Strike prick, too! A prick is part of a man. Cedric's like Pancho and Joselito. He offered to be the girl for me, back at the hacienda.

"Ahah!" Gaston laughed. "Hell hath no fury like a mariposa scorned! I'd heard the English gentry went for that sort of thing a lot."

Captain Gringo shook his head and said, "This is one time we don't get to blame Sir Basil Hakim and his *veddy veddy* friends in high places, unless old Cedric buys his arms from Woodbine Arms, of course. While I was in Padre Alejandro's library I had a gander at the *Almanac de Gotha*. You know what that is, Gaston?"

"But of course. I worked in a hotel one time, before I joined the legion to avoid meeting M'sieu de Paris and his *très* amusing guillotine. Every hotel in Paris keeps a copy of the *Almanac de Gotha* under its desk. Some people will put on airs as they travel, but the book has the titles of every noble family in Europe printed in black and white, non?"

"You got it. There isn't any Sir Cedric Neville in the *Almanac de Gotha* or *Burke's Peerage*. Padre Alejandro had both books. So the swish who tried to drown me is travelling under a false I.D. He didn't tell the customs men here in Belize he was any peer, either. They have their own books, and the Brits are sort of stuffy about saying you have an English title when you don't. They actually can make you pay a fine for pretending to be a nobleman or a British officer. Pam and Cecil probably put in here using their real names. It's tough to register a yacht without proper I.D., see?"

"Eh, bien, but in that case how are we to discover which yacht is theirs, and would you mind telling me what all this skullduggery with fake titles might be about?"

"Oh, that's obvious," Captain Gringo answered. "The act was to be taken as a harmless eccentric Sir, pottering about old Mayan ruins and all that rot. He wasn't looking for jewelry down in those cenotes. He was looking for what I found, a way into the cavern system under the limestone."

"*Merde alors*! Does that mean he acted as an advance scout for the mahogany pirates?"

"No. The mahogany pirates already knew how to float their illegal logs through the caves. Cedric's game was interrupted when the loggers rough methods caused the Indians to attack every white in the area they could find. He's not looking for an underground river. He wants an underground road. The guy's running guns to Guatemalan rebel factions. It's the only thing that works."

"We met no rebel guerrilla bands, Dick."

"Well of *course* we didn't, damn it! You have to have *guns* before you come out in the *open*! Cedric, and probably Pam, plan to move the guns in once they find a nice sneaky way, see?"

Gaston walked lighter as he laughed and said, "Ah, now I do not feel so shitty about stealing their yacht. We shall, of course, use it to get back to Puerto Barrios, after we deal with the steamer who ran us down, *non*?"

"Yeah, but don't count your chickens before they hatch, Gaston. A lot can still go wrong before we're finished, here."

"I wish you hadn't said that, Dick. You have this *très* rude habit of taking my words right out of my mouth!"

For once Captain Gringo didn't attract attention in a strange town with his Anglo-Saxon features. Everyone in Belize who wasn't black looked fairly Anglo-Saxon. The natives got even friendlier once he started buying the drinks in a seedy waterfront saloon.

He and Gaston told the other shabby-looking characters hanging about the docks and quays that they'd just come down from the high country after panning a little color. They'd have probably let him buy them drinks if he'd confessed to being Jack The Ripper.

The white strawboss of a black stevedore gang was "supervising" in the shade of the saloon. So Captain Gringo cooled him off some more with gin and tonic and soon established that the crew of the *Imperial Trader* were a "rum lot" who kept to themselves, but that most of the crew had gone somewhere up the Rio Belize in a steamlaunch towing a string of canoes, leaving a skeleton crew aboard the steamer with her surly skipper.

Meanwhile, Gaston had befriended a waterfront loafer who knew for a fact there was only one yacht moored down the quay with nobody on board, since he'd been hired to keep an eye on her. He said the "Hoity toity and his loity" who'd come in aboard the *Bird Of Passage* were named Chambers and that they'd gone inland on some sort of safari.

As the two soldiers of fortune headed back to Mammy Crawford's, Gaston said, "Eh bien, highjacking the yacht will be the making of duck soup. She is ketch rigged and has an engine as well, so the two of us can man her in the pinch. But from there on it becomes confusing. The *Bird Of Passage* is a sea-going yacht, not a gunboat. Your machinegun would no doubt make a *très* interesting line of dents in the steel plates of the *Imperial Trader*'s hull, but then what?"

"We'll have to board her and open the sea cocks to scuttle her, of course."

Gaston blanched and demanded, "*We*? You say *we*? *Mas non,* my Roger of the jolly madness! It is too big the boo! I do not doubt for a minute you could win a fire fight against overwhelming odds. But you forget the ship is moored under the protection of the British Empire! What happens when the on-shore police hear you making le boom boom boom, hein?"

"They'll probably come out to investigate, of course. That's why we'll want to hit-and-run in the dark of the moon. My almanac says the moon will set a little after four A.M. Good time, another way. Everybody will have turned in by that hour."

"Everyone but the deck-watch aboard the *Imperial Trader,* you mean! But very well, let us assume you can dispose of that wearisome detail. Let us assume the accursed ship is scuttled. What of it? The owners will simply salvage it and, voila, the *Imperial Trader* steams on again!"

Captain Gringo grimaced up at the sun, knowing they had a long day and most of a night to kill, and that he'd already laid all three adelitas. He said, "I don't care if they salvage her eventually. Or, yeah, I do care, but you can only do what you can do. The point is that the present skipper won't run down any more small craft, and at least we'll ruin her cargo."

"What cargo, Dick? We just saw to it that the *Imperial Trader* has no mahogany to leave with, this voyage."

"That was her *outbound* bill of lading. She was low in the water when she ran us down and she's moored out there now with her water-line just showing. Even unscrupulous owners like to carry cargo across the Atlantic both ways, right?"

"*Ah, oui,* but what do you suppose she had in her hold when she ran us down?"

"Something she didn't want to discuss with the local civil authorities, of course. If her papers only list Belize as a port of call, British Customs won't check out her hold. They're probably unloading her a little at a time, under cover of darkness. I said she was acting like a gun-runner when she left us down the coast to drown."

"But you said you didn't think Pam and Cedric Neville or Chambers, were with the gang, non?"

"So what? With a revolution brewing, all sorts of people will be running guns! Let's not worry about the loose ends. Let's just finish the bastards off!"

Cascadero was for the idea, when they told him about it back at Mammy Crawford's. The girls were dubious, but adelitas went where their soldados went, so what the hell. Lolita took Captain Gringo aside and asked him where they were going to fuck during the La Siesta. He said, "They don't go in for La Siesta in British Crown Colonies, so we have to stay on guard."

"I do not wish to stay on guard, Deek, I wish to fuck."

"Later. I'm sure there are separate staterooms aboard the yacht and we face a long cruise back to Puerto Barrios." He patted her on the rump and added, "Besides, there's no place to make love in private around here but that garbage dump."

Lolita reminded him she liked novelty, but he insisted they behave themselves. He'd probably find it novel to tear off a piece in a garbage dump, too, since it was about the only place he could recall where he'd never done so. But a guy sure would look silly at a time like that if someone came out from town with a wagonload of garbage.

By noon Mammy Crawford had told all their fortunes and said they'd drunk all her tea. So she said she'd go into town and buy some more. Captain Gringo waited until the old conjure woman was out of sight before he turned to the others and said, "All right, troops. Time to move out on the double. We'll bee-line for the woods and circle to the far side of town for openers."

Nobody but Gaston questioned his orders. As they left, packing the few things they really needed, Gaston said, "Eh bien, *I* noticed that sealed cannister of tea on the top shelf, too! How soon should the police arrive at the shanty back there, my old and suspicious?"

Captain Gringo shrugged and said, "Depends on how seriously they take her story. She doesn't really have anything on us. The cops may wonder why a couple of beachcombers and their native friends are skulking around the garbage dump. Then again, they may not. We can't take the chance."

"I agree. But where do you suggest we go? We don't know the town. Lurking anywhere will seem as suspicious, non?"

"Yeah. We'd better get aboard the yacht. It's the last place anyone would expect such a scruffy bunch to be. We'll walk down the quay from the far end and simply go aboard like a cleaning crew or something. There's only one guy who's supposed to be keeping an eye on the yacht, remember?"

"*Oui,* and we left him *très* drunk in the saloon. But can we count on him being so derelict in his duties for so many hours, Dick?"

"No. As soon as we get the girls and Cascadero on board you'd better go and get him. You're the guy he drinks with. Buy him a few more, then ask him to show you around the yacht, see?"

"Ah, and when I bring him aboard where you and Cascadero are lurking, that will be the end of him, hein?"

Captain Gringo shook his head and said, "No. In the first place that would be shifty. In the second, we can use him if anyone else comes to nose around. Everyone knows he was left in charge of the yacht, right?"

"Eh bien, but what if he does not wish to join us, Dick?"

"Then we kill him. But I don't think we'll have to. He's just a down-on-his-heels drifter. He's obviously spent the money Pam and Cedric gave him, since he's bumming drinks. We've got plenty of booze in our packs and if he likes sex, we can supply that, too."

"*Merde alors,* just as I was getting to know Ynez, too! I don't think it would be a good idea to take Juanita away from our black compadre, Cascadero. You, of course, are attached to Lolita?"

"We'll work it out. If we have to, to keep him happy, we'll ask the girls to take turns screwing him blind."

The so-called watchman of the *Bird Of Passage* solved
the problem in the end by being more interested in booze
than broads. He said his name was 'Arry and that he came
from Liverpool and loved them all, whoever they were. He
was too drunk to grasp any explanations, so Captain
Gringo didn't give him any. They put him in the forward
cabin with the girls taking turns, not screwing him, but
keeping him supplied with booze.

Captain Gringo took over the master cabin, found it
was luxurious and had soft twin bunks, side-by-side, and
killed some of the daylight hours with Lolita when 'Arry
passed out and only needed one girl at a time to stand
watch over him. Lolita insisted on trying both bunks and
the plush carpeting between them. The other two guys
with him got to explore their own cabins when he sent
Lolita back on duty, looking very serene.

There were canned goods in the galley. ('Arry had of
course drunk all the booze in the bar by now to keep it
from falling into the hands of thieves.) So they ate,
lounged around, and managed to kill the day and half the
night. Captain Gringo fired the oil burning boiler amid
ships at midnight, to build up a full head of steam. Then,
at four in the morning they cast off.

The skilled Cascadero manned the helm. The three girls
stood forward with the Winchesters they'd been issued as

well as their orders. As they steamed slowly out to the *Imperial Trader*, the bigger vessel's super-structure was visible because of her oil-burning deck lights. The hull was only a black mass that *Bird Of Passage* would be invisible against from the shore. Captain Gringo spotted a gap in the rails and told Cascadero, "Make for the foot of her sea ladder. Ease off on the throttle so we don't bump hard with our bow. But then give her some power and hold her nose against the hull."

Cascadero nodded and said, "I know the plan, My Captain."

Gaston snorted and asked, "You call this madness a plan?"

"Gaston," Captain Gringo said, "I want you covering me from down here with the machinegun, okay?"

"I certainly had no intention of boarding that monster! But what about you, Dick? One can see you are big, but they say there are at least a dozen in that skeleton crew, and you don't know the layout of the ship as they do!"

"They don't know I'm coming, either. A three-island freighter is a three-island freighter. How complicated can it be, topside?"

Cascadero closed the throttle. Captain Gringo nodded and moved forward as Gaston muttered, "It was nice knowing you Dick."

Captain Gringo hefted the 12 Gauge pumpgun he'd taken from the supplies and as the blunt bowsprit nudged between the rungs of the ship's ladder with a soft bump, he ran along the sprit like a squirrel, shotgun in one hand, and caught the ladder. He went up it, took a deep breath, and rolled through the gap in the rails, glancing anxiously both ways.

There was nobody on deck within sight. But as he rose, he heard footsteps. He slid into the inky shadow of an air vent against the cabin bulkhead.The steps grew louder. A guy wearing a knit cap and a pistol belt came into view, sauntering along the rail with a bored expression. Then he must have spotted the masts of *Bird Of Passage* against thet shore lights.

He moved over to the rail and looked down. But before he could shout, Captain Gringo dashed out and caved in the back of his skull with the butt plate of his shotgun. He dragged the body out of sight and found an unlocked entrance to the superstructure. Inside, it was dimly lit by another lantern at the far end of the companionway. He moved down it on the balls of his feet, ears as well as shotgun cocked. He found a stairwell running down into the hold. So he followed it down to see what they were carrying down there that made them too important to stop for drowning men.

The hold was filled with boxes. It was pretty dim down there, so he struck a match. The lettering on the nearest crates said it was full of farm machinery. He couldn't see hacienda that used peon labor needing much in the way of modern machinery, so he pried open a crate. Then he quickly shook out the match. It wasn't a good idea to hold a lit match over barrels of gunpowder!

But as he waited for his nerves to calm down, he grinned. He didn't have to search further for any fucking sea cocks.

Putting the shotgun aside as he worked, Captain Gringo took out his pocket knife and removed his worn shirt. He spread the cloth on a crate and began to carve out a long strip of cloth, cutting out from the middle in a spiral so as to wind up with almost twenty feet of sunbaked, sweat-stained cotton. Even with his body oils impregnated in the fibers it would burn slowly. But it would burn, and he sure didn't want it to burn fast!

He stuck one end of his improvised fuse in the tap hole of a black powder barrel, grateful for the primitive firearms a lot of people still used down here in bananaland. Then he picked up his shotgun and backed to the ladderway, uncoiling his improvised slow fuse. It almost reached. He struck another match, lit the safe end, and departed posthaste.

The ringing of his boots on the steel treads couldn't be helped. This was no time for pussy-footing. As he got back up to the companionway, a door opened and a man wearing four stripes on his sleeves called out, "What's going on out here? Who are you? What are you doing aboard my vessel?"

Captain Gringo blew him off his feet with a shotgun blast as he muttered, "Haven't time to talk. I really must be going."

Then he went. The roar of the shotgun of course woke up the whole ship. But he was going down the ladder before anyone could do much about it. As he leaped for the bow of *Bird Of Passage* he yelled, "Full steam astern!" and by the time he got back to Gaston and Cascadero in the cockpit, *Bird Of Passage* was backing away nicely.

Then a rifle squibbed aboard *Imperial Trader* and the bullet thunked into the teak deck of the yacht too close for comfort. So Captain Gringo shoved Gaston away from the breech of the Maxim, snapping, "What the fuck were you waiting for?" As he swung the muzzle and elevated it to train it on the long row of heads peering over the rail of the steamer at them!

He opened up, traversing the length of the rail with spitting death as Cascadero, without being told, reversed the engine and sheered away. Captain Gringo didn't know how many he'd hit and how many had just ducked behind the steel bulwarks. The point was academic. He ceased fire, shoved Cascadero away from the wheel, and gave them hard right rudder at full speed as he called out, "Everybody hit the deck and stay there!"

So they did and Captain Gringo had his back to the steamer, crouching low, as the whole harbor was illuminated in hell-fire orange and windows shattered a quarter mile inland!

Aside from sounding like they were right inside a thunderclap, the shock wave booted *Bird Of Passage* in the ass and slammed Captain Gringo against the wheel. But as he straightened up in the sudden darkness, none of his ribs seemed to be broken after all, so what the hell.

Gaston sat up, ears ringing, and muttered, "Yo ho ho and boom boom boom indeed! How did you *do* that, Dick?"

"Gunpowder. Someone's plotting a real uprising of the masses. Major Llamas will be interested to know a mess of disgruntled peons figure to be marching on the capital with their grandfather's cap and ball muskets."

Gaston took out a smoke, lit it, and said, "I think he already knows that, Dick. You're not still seriously considering a return to Puerto Barrios, are you?"

Captain Gringo turned his head to gaze shoreward. Lights were going on and people were running up and down a lot, but he knew they were not visible, running out to sea with no lights showing. He said, "Keep that smoke down below the rail. What are you talking about, Gaston? We have to go back to get *paid,* don't we?"

Gaston snorted in disgust and replied, "*Merde alors,* he steals a luxury yacht, worth God-knows-how-much, and he discusses day wages! Haven't we been wondering why they sent us and a rag-tag assortment of half-asses to investigate the rumors about mahogany pirates, Dick? Major Llamas has a regular army at his disposal, non?"

"Hmm, I see what you mean. Okay, he heard rumors about an impending revolution. So he wanted to keep his regulars near at hand if and when the balloon went up."

"Or," Gaston pointed out, "the major and his men are in on the coming revolt and did not wish to miss the main action when the central government ordered him to look into the maghogany business, hein?"

Captain Gringo nodded as the first ground swells of the open seas swayed the duckboards under him. He said, "It could work either way. If the major's legit, he means to pay us. If he was using us for dupes . . . "

"Exactly, Dick. Is it worth going back to find out, the hard way?" Captain Gringo thought. Then, as the girls came aft to join them, he grinned and said, "No, Pam and Cecil won't miss this yacht until they get down to the coast

191

again. By then we'll have unloaded it in Costa Rica for a lot more than Guatemala owes us. Meanwhile, we've got booze and broads and all the food we can possibly eat. Cascadero and the girls will like it just as well in Costa Rica, and I don't think 'Arry cares where he is, as long as he can stay drunk. So, okay, this time Guatemala gets our services on the house. Next stop Costa Rica!"

Gaston was so delighted he offered to stand the first watch at the wheel. Captain Gringo patted Cascadero on the back and told him to turn in with Juanita. As he headed for his own cabin, the tall black Lolita and the tiny Ynez joined him on either side. "Ynez and me just thought of a new game," Lolita said. "Would you like to join us?"

He grinned and replied, "Why not? I don't have to take the wheel for at least four hours, and I don't feel sleepy at all."